The Eater
of Darkness

By
Robert M. Coates

City Point Press

Publishing history:

Originally published by Contact Editions, Paris, 1926.

Reprinted by the Macauley Company, New York, 1929.

Published with a new introduction by the author by

G.P. Putnam's Sons, New York, 1959.

New edition copyright © David Wilk 2021

Foreword copyright © by Mathilde Roza 2021

Paperback ISBN 978-1-947951-23-5

eBook ISBN 978-1-947951-22-8

Cover and book design by Barbara Aronica-Buck

Cover art from iStockphoto/duncan1890

Printed in Canada

Published by

City Point Press

PO Box 2063

Westport CT 06880

(203) 571-0781

www.citypointpress.com

CONTENTS

The Eater of Darkness

by Robert M. Coates

!?

$1.15
$1.25
in
Canada

Iwould be both a fool and a liar if I didn't admit straightaway that I'm delighted to see this first book of mine re-published. If the first novel is like the first-born child—and it is, for it is always regarded a little more tenderly and forgivingly than the ones that follow—then it seems to me that the same novel, re-issued, is a little like the appearance of the first grand-child. There is the same sense of being at one remove, combining the pleasures of parenthood without its pains and anxieties, and the same respectful feeling that one is involved, despite one's self, in the ancient processes of continuity; and the easy, irresponsible fondness—most of all, perhaps, the feeling of irresponsibility. "I didn't write the thing," the grandfather-author says. "If anyone's to blame, blame him," and ignoring the paradox in time he points to his spiritual son, that youngster in his twenties, back there.

There is also that grandfatherly tendency to lean back and reminisce. Can you spare me a moment or two while I light my pipe? Then I'll tell you about the early and middle nineteen-twenties—or as we call them, the good old days.

To begin with, this book was written in what I am convinced were happier, more hopeful and confident times than we are likely to see again for many, many years. Every age, every generation, in its youth, has its problems, its trials, its triumphs and its uncertainties. We had ours. But apart from all this mine had also the glorious feeling that we were truly on the threshold of a Golden Age. We had it on the highest authority that the last great war, the War To End Wars, had been fought—hadn't even President Wilson said so?—and we believed it. And not only we, but a good share of our elders believed it too; I can still remember the outcries of horror and condemnation that swept the world when Laurence Stallings published that massive compilation of war photographs, around 1925, and titled it "The First World War." "First World War," indeed! There was fighting going on here and there sporadically, of course: in the Riff, against Abd El Krim, and mysterious doings in Russia; the Japanese were beginning to throw their weight around in Manchuria. But that there would ever be another Great War-*that* was unthinkable; surely we had all learned our lesson about that!

Stallings was right, of course, and already there were forces slowly gaining strength and direction which would eventually justify his ironic prediction. But I won't go into them here, for we didn't know about them. The young men of my generation looked forward to peace, to peace timeless, unhurried and indestructible; I would suggest that you pause for a moment, as I sometimes do, to think about that, and compare the basic outlook it suggests with the mixture of frustration, anxiety and downright fear that lies in the back of every man's mind nowadays when he picks up his morning paper or turns on the radio.

This fact, too, I think, had a great deal to do with creating the atmosphere of the period—a mixture of optimism, enthusiasm and feverish activity. It was a fine time to be young in, especially in Paris and for a bunch of kids from Pittsburgh, Cincinnati, Rochester, Dallas and other way stations who until the war had hardly known Europe existed. It was the Dada period, and for me Dada has always meant gaiety: the one artistic movement I know of whose main purpose was having fun. It was also a period of experimentation. There was indeed a ferment in all the arts, and in the field of literature we had three titans leading the way—Gertrude Stein, James Joyce and Ezra Pound—who in their separate fashions were manipulating the English language in ways that had never been done before; and if the headiness of all this made us sometimes a little punch-drunk or just plain silly it must, I think, be conceded that we were honestly so.

Unlike the present "beat" generation, which sometimes seems to me to be playing both ends against the middle, we felt that if we were in revolt, we could neither give quarter to the enemy nor accept it. We were so far out, as the saying goes now, that success distressed us. Our "little" magazines—*Broom, Gargoyle, Secession, transition*, and so on—remained determinedly little, eschewing anything so vulgar as wide circulation and financial profits; while a good review, if it came from one of the pooh-bahs of the period, was equally disturbing. Praise from such a quarter could only mean that you had slipped up somewhere, and I still remember my uneasiness when an early book of mine, "The Outlaw Years," *was* successful: what had I done, I wondered, to deserve such loathsome encomiums? (One of the French Dadaists, Louis Aragon—now oddly enough, a leading figure in the Communist party over there, and presumably with no time for such nonsense—went so far as to write the book editors of the Paris papers individually, promising to horsewhip them if they so much as mentioned his new book. Most of us had our parents to support us, of course—or to help, as mine did, while I earned a little money on the side—and the cost of living, owing to the exchange, as almost embarrassingly low. My average income, from all sources, was about fifty dollars a month, and I certainly never felt deprived.)

This book, though it wasn't an actual flop, had a gratifying lack of success in the proper quarters, and a pleasantly comforting *succès d'estime* elsewhere. The fact is that I'd honestly never expected to see it in published in the first place, so in a sense anything I got out of it was gravy. My attitude at the time was a confused, variable and thoroughly jejune mixture of Francois Villon (the medieval influence, and also general rascality, though a more law-abiding rascal than I was in those days could hardly be imagined); Sir Philip Sidney (the great sixteenth-century English poet, representing the aristocratic impulse) and Dada, or devil-may-careness. In this instance, it was largely Sidney's influence that governed me.

Like many of his high-born contemporaries, he never stooped to seek out a publisher for his writings. He just had a fair copy of them made and circulated among his friends, and

I figured that if that was the way Sidney did things, why, so would I. I was back in New York for a year, trying to recoup, or perhaps simply coup my finances (after all, I couldn't depend on my family forever) when the early part of the book was written. But I finished it in Giverny, a lovely small Seine-side town about fifty miles down the river from Paris—having managed, more or less by the skin of my teeth, to get back to France again—and Giverny, though fundamentally a farm village, and a charming one, had been a resort for artists and writers ever since Claude Monet had settled there some fifty years earlier.

He was still living there, the patriarch of the place, as he was of the whole Impressionist movement; and so, by that time, was a grandson, another artist, half French and half American, named James Butler. Jim was also a dabbler in all sorts of hand-icrafts, and the purpose of this long digression, nostalgic as it is to me, is to say that when the book was finished I simply typed it off carefully, and with Jim's help managed to bind it fairly neatly—and thought that would be the end of it. Or not quite the end, for there still remained the gentlemanly circulariza-tion of friends; and one of the friends, and a particularly dear one, whom I tapped in this manner, was Gertrude Stein. She read it, and liked it, and immediately set about getting it pub-lished. Though I may have yawned delicately at the prospect, I must admit now that I was pretty darned pleased at the way things were turning out. I can see now that a good deal of my disdain at the idea of mingling art with commerce, like a good many of our other attitudes of the period, was basically simply hedging: I wasn't at all sure that anybody was going to want to publish the thing in the first place.

I have my reservations about parts of the book now, but have made relatively few changes. I have changed, or tried to clarify a few references that were so personal or so much of the period that they'd be needlessly cryptic now, but otherwise I have made no effort to "bring it up to date."* There *were* Elevateds in New York then, and they did cost a nickel a ride; there was vaudeville, and the movies were silent and had captions; girls (God bless them) did wear a chemise; and Giverny (God bless it too) though now almost a suburb of Paris, was then so quietly rural at night that you *could* hear the old water mill on the river nearby throbbing "so soft it might be thunder in Constantinople."

I have tampered with a couple passages that really grieved me, but I've left others that are equally improvable if they seemed to require more ambitious changes. Though it's probably the most "personal" of all, I've left the voluminous dedication as it is, for sentimental reasons. It was intended, in a kind of grab-bag way, as a tribute to friends and other persons or organizations who had helped in one way or another in the book's production. Robert McAlmon, for instance, who was getting out Contact Editions in Paris, at considerable cost to his own writing, was the book's first publisher; Nick Carter, "Sapper" and Fantômas, their French equivalent, were among the writers of thrillers on whom the book was modeled. The *New York Times* comes on the list because its Sunday magazine section was a welcome customer for the "color" stories I wrote (odd corners of New York, and even odder corners of Paris, and so on) which helped finance it, and Gerald Chapman was a bank robber and gunman very much in the news at the time . . . perhaps that's enough to give the general idea.

As I've said, Gertrude Stein, who is also mentioned in the dedication, was the one who practically *got* the book published; but she was a help, a support and an encourager in ways that went beyond that. One wonderful thing about the nineteen-twenties in Paris, as I look back on them, was that the "great ones," even the titans, were so accessible. You didn't have to make an appointment, and a pilgrimage, to meet Léger, Picasso, Satie, Pascin, Juan Gris, Tristan Tzara or Brancusi, to mention a few names at random. You found them sitting at a table nearby on the *terrasse* of the Café du Dome, the Select or the Rôtonde, in the Montparnasse Quarter, or the Deux Magôts in the Saint-Germain, and as the evening wore on and mutual friends appeared you were likely to find yourself sitting at the same table with them, or as their table indefinitely rounded out, satellite, with other tables— and talking and drinking with them without the least self-consciousness on either side.

Brancusi was a great party-giver and so in those days was Pound, and at both their houses there was the same feeling of equality between the older and more established artists and the young newcomers. In a sense, the atmosphere has always seemed to me a little like that of the Cripple Creek gold-mining district, where I lived for a while as a boy: with everyone striving for new strikes or new discoveries, anyone might strike it rich, and meanwhile there was room for all.

James Joyce was an exception, being more retiring, and so was Gertrude Stein, who just didn't like the randomness of café life. A big woman, calm, massive-faced, massive-bodied, with a brown Italian coloring that was accentuated by her habit of wearing loose-woven peasant-like skirts and blouses, and sandals, she lived with her life-long friend, Alice Toklas (darker, wirier and more active) in the famous apartment, 27 rue de Fleurus, off the Luxembourg Gardens, and in a sense presided there. I think now that she may have felt a certain frustration herself, for in her lifetime she never got (has not got even now) the recognition that was due her for her influence in introducing an almost mathematical lucidity (the classic influence, as distinguished from Joyce's, the romantic influence) into the treatment of the English language.

At any rate, people came to her, not she to them— Sherwood Anderson, Thornton Wilder, Ernest Hemingway, among many others—and though a few of them, notably Hemingway, disavowed her later, I think most of us remember and treasure the warmth, the understanding and (again) the feeling of artistic equality we got from her.

I won't go further into that, though, for I feel I'm in danger of getting soppy, and I've certainly talked enough about myself. Instead, I'd like to use the space remaining to me to add one more anecdote to the annals of Steiniana. I'll make it as brief as possible. We'd got talking one day about Anthony Trollope, who was one of her great admirations, and when I'd confessed I'd never read him, she promised casually to send me some books of his. A few days later an expressman delivered, not a parcel, but a carton, a crate full, heavy with books—with Trollope, in short: the Barchester series, the Parliamentary series, practically all of him, and as you probably know all of Trollope means a great deal of reading indeed.

I was wading in Trollope for months, I was practically drunk with him, for I discovered that I loved him too. But I still feel that if you're going to get to know Trollope, that's the way to do it, and the way Gertrude handled the matter is typical of the largeness of her own nature, too.

Robert M. Coates, 1959

Drawing by Robert M. Coates, early 1920s. (Robert M. Coates papers,
American Heritage Center, Laramie, WY)

INTRODUCTION TO THE 2021 EDITION
Mathilde Roza

T*he Eater of Darkness*, published in Paris in 1926, is a unique avant-garde novel. Since its appearance, it has been termed "one of the most unusual literary concoctions of the period," a "melodramatic extravaganza of the most nonsensical sort," "one of the cleverest tours de force ever contrived by the pen of a wit," and "a hilariously misconstructed hurricane of happenstance, adventure and parody."[1] Most famously, following the publication of the novel in New York in 1929, *The Eater of Darkness* became known as the first Dada novel in English. Because of the occurrence of a futuristic and sinister x-ray machine in its plot, the novel is also recognized as an important early science fiction novel in encyclopedias of the genre. The novel, in short, has much to offer and deserves recognition as a rare and inspiring product of the spirit of creativity that ignited the early 1920s.

The book's author was Robert Myron Coates, a young American who had come to the French capital five years before. Coates had been born in New Haven in 1897. He was the only child of Harriet Coates, a middle-class Victorian with feminist sympathies, and Frederick Coates, a machinist with a fascination for inventions. During his career Frederick gradually developed from a toolmaker to a designer of special

WEST SIDE CYCLERY,

FRED. COATES, Prop.

Agent for Fine Bicycles, Suits, Caps,
Sundries, etc.
        Sole Agent for

Humber, Duquesne, Winchester, Standard and Coronet Bicycles.

First-Class Repairing.   Special attention paid to
working up Inventions.

93 CONGRESS AVE., NEW HAVEN, CONN.

Frederick Coates's bicycle store, 1897. In New Haven, Frederick Coates provided for the family by running a bicycle store. Note the reference to "working up inventions." (New Haven Museum and Historical Society, New Haven city directory, 1897)

machinery. The American literary critic Malcolm Cowley, thinking of Robert Coates's strong drive toward literary experimentation, once linked him to the senior Coates, writing: "I think of [Robert Coates] as a craftsman, an inspired mechanic working with words as his father had worked with pieces of metal, choosing and calibrating, fitting together, then grinding and polishing in the hope of achieving some ultimate invention."[2] Frederick Coates's career certainly had a significant impact on the author's youth; between 1905 and 1915 the small family traveled the country, settling down in various gold-mining districts in Colorado and then in Seattle, Portland, Cincinnati, Springfield, Buffalo, New York City, Rochester, and other places. As a result, the young Coates never lived in one place for a long period of time. He attended countless different schools and always, as he wrote in his memoirs, he was "for a period at least, the new boy, the outsider."[3] In 1915 he enrolled at Yale University (Class of 1919) and became a frequent contributor to the *Yale Literary Magazine*, joining the magazine's editorial board in his senior year. When World War I broke out, he enrolled in the Yale R.O.T.C. (Reserve Officers Training Corps) to become a pilot, but the war was over before he had obtained his wings. After graduation, Coates moved to New York. Drawn there by a great love and fascination for the city, he embarked on a career in advertising, but his heart was not in it; he longed to go abroad and become a writer.

Drawing by Robert Coates of himself in a Paris bar, 1921. From Paris, Coates sent a letter to his friend Reginald Marsh that included a drawing Marsh might have made of him, "This is you in Paris." (Archives of American Art, Reginald Marsh Papers)

With money from his father, Coates sailed to France in 1921, at a time when expatriation was fast becoming a generational trend. As a result, the writer later complained, he "automatically became an 'exile' and a part of the 'Lost Generation.'"4 In Paris, he found lodgings on 9 La Rue de la Grande Chaumière, just off the Boulevard du Montparnasse, in the heart of the bohemian American Quarter. He thoroughly enjoyed the Quarter's boisterous and unpredictable café life, and especially loved the congenial artistic climate that he encountered there; in fact, Paris reminded him of the Cripple Creek gold-mining district in Colorado where he had lived as a boy. In both places, he later wrote in his memoirs, "with everyone striving for new strikes or new discoveries, anyone might strike it rich, and meanwhile there was room for all."5 In France, he established meaningful contacts with literary figures such as Arthur Moss, Florence Gilliam, Matthew Josephson, Malcolm Cowley, Ernest Hemingway, Kathleen Cannell, Harold Loeb, Ford Madox Ford, and Laurence Vail, and published highly experimental prose sketches in the expatriate little magazines *Gargoyle*, *Broom*, and *Secession*. He developed a special relationship with Gertrude Stein, the matriarch of modernism, who owned the famous *salon* on 27 Rue de Fleurus. In fact, according to Stein's biographer, Coates had been "a Rue-de-Fleurus favorite."6

In the fall of 1923, Coates temporarily returned to New York City and, like the protagonist of *The Eater of Darkness*, Charles Dograr, settled down in a rooming house on West 23rd Street. There, he started working on the manuscript that would become *The Eater of Darkness.* Returning to France exactly one year later, again like Dograr, he settled down in the village of Giverny, finished the manuscript in 1925, and circulated it among his friends. Two of these, Kathleen Cannell and Gertrude Stein, brought the manuscript to the attention of American expatriate publisher Robert McAlmon—who, by that time, had published work by Ernest Hemingway, Marsden Hartley, William Carlos Williams, Ford Madox Ford, Ezra Pound, H.D., and Mary Butts. McAlmon accepted the book for publication, and *The Eater of Darkness* appeared as a Contact Edition in 1926.

In terms of plot, *The Eater of Darkness* revolves around the adventures of Charles Dograr, who has recently left France, abandoning his French lover, to spend a year in New York. Dograr's exploits commence when, one night, he leaves his boarding house room and haphazardly wanders into the quarters of a macabre old man (Picrolas) who calls himself "the Eater of Darkness." Picrolas, whose body is covered with geometrical formulae and equations, is the inventor of a machine that emits far-traveling x-ray beams, so-called "x-ray bullets." To his horrified amazement, Charles discovers that the machine is designed to kill random individuals by electrocuting their brains from a great distance. We will not here reveal the novel's plot, but what follows is, in Coates's own words, "a moviesque hodge-podge of murder, armored cars, x-ray bullets and bank hold-ups."[7] It contains many surprises and confusions for the reader.

More than any other literary work that came out of this

period, *The Eater of Darkness* is a reflection and celebration of the time and the place in which it was conceived and provides a humorous panorama of the inspiring and bewildering climate of transatlantic modernism. Taking the role of participant-observer, Coates produced something akin to a literary seismogram, a record of the shifts, movements, and disturbances created by modernity and a collage-like catalogue of the many new ways in which art responded to modernity's new demands. Modernity brought a new intensity and speed of life, groundbreaking scientific insights and inventions, greater complexity, mechanization, new social mores, and the rise of advertising and mass culture, as well as a rapidly growing enjoyment of popular culture, especially silent movies and pulp magazines. Art exploded into a myriad of "-isms," from Cubism, Expressionism, Futurism, Constructivism, and Imagism to Dadaism and surrealism; new possibilities were constantly invented, tested, and debated; and the turmoil was such that Coates felt that living in Paris during the 1920s was like living in a cultural war zone. As he wrote in 1955:

"In the twenties, a cheerful combativeness was the rule, and the rows over matters of the minutest dogma reached fantastic proportions. There were schools within schools, and factions within factions . . . all splitting up, warring briefly, and uniting again with such furious rapidity that it was advisable for the outsider (and the American, to a certain extent, was inevitably an outsider; we just didn't have the Frenchman's capacity for exuberant contentiousness) to keep a constant check on the disposition of forces, a sort of daily war map, if he wanted to make his way through the melee without embarrassment."[8]

Next to the novel's collage-like aspect, Coates's pioneering use of popular culture in fiction is particularly striking. Coates had always been interested in popular culture—as his early writings for the *Yale Literary Magazine* attest—but the European avant-garde's embrace of (American) popular culture proved liberating in the extreme; in addition to silent movies, *The Eater of Darkness* mediates popular literary genres like science fiction, the hard-boiled detective, the murder mystery, Nick Carter novels, and the French detective thriller series about the arch-criminal Fantômas. As the book approaches its resolution, the narrative is occasionally rendered through cinematic techniques, including the reproduction of silent movie captions. At other moments, Coates taps into the world of pulp fiction to tie the novel's various narrative threads together "as unscrupulously as any hack employed to manufacture Street & Smith paper-backed classics,"[9] as Robert Sage described the novel's "melodramadness" in his review for the literary journal *transition*. The anarchic and ingenuous nature of *The Eater of Darkness* was not lost on the book reviewers. In Paris, the book elicited the wrath of *Paris Tribune* critic Alex Small, noted for his low regard of American Left Bank activity, who demanded to know how much longer "intelligent people in the Quarter [would] be bullied by the sort of stuff and nonsense that Mr. Coates has the infernal cheek to put into print."[10] In other quarters the novel received high praise, for instance from Elliot

Paul, the future co-editor of *transition*, who focused on Coates's skills as a satirist, discovering stylistic parodies of James Joyce, Waldo Frank, E. E. Cummings, Sherwood Anderson, Jean Toomer, Max Bodenheim, Frank Harris, and Ben Hecht.

It took three years for *The Eater of Darkness* to be published in New York. It appeared in 1929, with the Macaulay Publishing Company, in a slightly altered edition: among other things, the 1929 text features more parentheses, reflecting Coates's style; a slightly different dedication page; and a shorter list of items that the x-ray beam travels through. The book had been accepted by Macaulay with the help of Coates's friend Ford Madox Ford, and was marketed as a literary sensation: "Since Ernest Hemingway," the dust jacket read, "no writer has been as much spoken of by the literary cognoscenti as Robert Coates." On the book's wraparound band, Ford pronounced the book to be "not the first but the best Dada novel," while Malcolm Cowley, another friend from Coates's Paris days, hailed the novel as "the first purely Dada novel to be published in English." Seizing on Ford's and Cowley's words, reviewers repeated the tag and the label stuck.

There can be no doubt that Dada, and its successor surrealism, were among Coates's central inspirations. The novel's light treatment of violence and death, the use of unmotivated crime, and the treatment of the urban-technological environment and the machine all comply with the French Dada and surrealist state of mind. Also, the deliberate lack of logic and rationality in the novel's plot, the consistent efforts to undermine interpretation,

● The Eater of Darkness
by Robert M. Coates

Since Ernest Hemingway no writer has been as much spoken of by the literary cognoscenti as Robert Coates. His book has literally been prayed for—and here it is fulfilling as well, the prayers of all who watch for civilized literary entertainment.

One can't describe it any more than one can describe a dynamo, Al Jolson, or a really beautiful woman. One can hint. . . .

* that it's a murder mystery so profound that it requires in addition to the usual detectives, and amateurs, the aid of science, and footnotes,

* that it has a scientist villain with logarithmic tables tatooed on his thighs and abstruser mathematics elsewhere on his body,

* that the ladies include a Parisian model, a dancer (Sweet Adeline) and a fille de joie (honorably and hopelessly in love),

* that the scene kaleidoscopes from Paris, all over New York, and (not too long) in Hoboken, Erie, etc.,

* that every situation in mystery fiction, and some new ones perform for our delight,

* and that only Lewis Carroll, writing for adults could have given us anything so hilariously, gracefully and logically mad as Bob Coates's EATER OF DARKNESS.

Macaulay
Publishers ● New York

From the dust jacket, The Eater of Darkness, *Macaulay Publishers, New York, 1929* and the author's heavy use of the devices of popular culture show a distinctly avant-gardist disdain for the traditions of High Art. Also, in writing *The Eater of Darkness*, Coates carried on the banner for Dadaist prose—a genre neglected by the Dadaists themselves—by stepping into the footsteps of Alfred Jarry, a writer who was admired by the Dadaists and acknowledged as an important precursor. *The Eater of Darkness* certainly builds on the styles and types of content that could be found in Jarry's *Exploits and Opinions of Doctor Faustroll, Pataphysician.* Among many other things, Jarry's work features a detailed elaboration of the science of "pataphysics," including geometrical hypotheses and algebraic equations. This theory cannot but recall Coates's mock-scientific exposé on the workings of the x-ray machine, outlined in the pages of *The Eater of Darkness* by the inventor, who believes he might be "the only *homo physico-philosophicus* in the history of man."

Despite its many Dada features, *The Eater of Darkness* is more than a Dada novel. As Arthur Moss, the editor of *Gargoyle*, wrote in his foreword to the 1926 edition: "It is not so easy to pigeonhole Robert Coates. . . . Coates is a lone wolf. It may even be that he is a young Mahomet, blazing his own new religion."[11] Perhaps it is best to treasure *The Eater of Darkness* as a celebration of the forces of human creativity. Among the remarkable results that Coates reaped by giving his novel up to these forces was a strikingly pre-postmodern element: throughout the novel Coates allows these powers to explicitly create and shape the world that he presents to the reader.

From the practice of daydreaming to the murder mystery; from the art of writing, weaving, or sculpting to the captions of a silent film; from the avant-garde manifesto to the tabloid; from technology and science to the ravings of a madman, all forms of creativity are set loose and acknowledged as co-creators by Robert Coates, even "Mr. Coates" himself (see Coates's footnote 4 to Chapter XI). The "license to create" is absolute.

Following *The Eater of Darkness*, Coates produced two more novels in which the question of how to write continued to guide his work. Both *Yesterday's Burdens* (1933) and *The Bitter Season* (1946) share the first novel's ambition to encapsulate a specific cultural time and place in suitable literary forms and styles, allowing each novel to emerge from the time that it seeks to document. *The Eater of Darkness* represented Paris and New York City in the early 1920s; *Yesterday's Burdens* presents New York and the Connecticut countryside in the early 1930s. *The Bitter Season*, a presciently confessional novel, summons up wartime New York City during the period leading up to D-Day while also outlining the painful processes of a divorce. After this "trilogy," Coates changed direction and began to focus on writing crime novels. The first of these, *Wisteria Cottage: A Novel of Criminal Impulse* (1948), was a psychological novel, highly intense in execution, and a popular success. The novel contains several unusual stylistic elements, but overall, Coates's experimentalism was much less pronounced. His second crime novel, the closely observed *The Farther Shore* (1955), was written in the naturalist vein and was the writer's last long piece of fiction.

During the 1960s, Coates produced a book of memoirs —*The View from Here*, in 1960—and two travel books about Italy.

During his lifetime, Coates was best known through his parallel career at the *New Yorker*, whose staff he joined in 1927, shortly after his "exile's return." Coates was associated with the magazine during most of his entire writing life, and developed friendships with several of the *New Yorker*'s editors and associates, among them James Thurber, Harold Ross, E. B. and Katharine White, Dorothy Parker, Janet Flanner, Wolcott Gibbs, St. Clair McKelway, Gus Lobrano, Russell Maloney, Ann Honeycutt, Sid Perelman, and later, William Maxwell and Brendan Gill. According to *New Yorker* scholar Ben Yagoda, Coates wrote more words for the magazine than anyone else, with the possible exception of Wolcott Gibbs and E. B. White. Starting out as a writer for the editorial "Talk of the Town," he contributed journalistic essays and profiles, humorous sketches, book reviews, and more than a hundred short stories, several of which were republished in prize anthologies. As a short-story writer, Coates played a significant role in the *New Yorker*'s development of a new type of modern, more truthful short story. Dealing with such somber themes as murder, violence, suicide, loneliness, humiliation, and moral failure, his psychologically dark stories of the 1930s and 1940s helped broaden the *New Yorker*'s category of the allowable in terms of subject matter. Finally, Coates was the magazine's art critic from 1937 to 1967, coining the term "abstract expressionism" in 1946.

Based on his many contributions to American letters,

Robert M. Coates, Gaylordsville, Connecticut, early 1930s. In 1930, Coates published a successful historical novel of the land pirates of the American Old Southwest, The Outlaw Years. With the prize money from the American Literary Guild, Coates was able to buy a house in Gaylordsville and moved there in 1931. (Photo courtesy of Mrs. Ingrid Waldron)

Coates was elected to the National Institute of Arts and Letters in 1958, but his reputation soon faded into oblivion. May the republication of *The Eater of Darkness*, more than sixty years after the novel's last republication in 1959 by Capricorn Press, contribute to a rediscovery of Coates's intriguing experimentalism and his multifaceted literary career. Its reappearance is a happy event, as well as a necessary one. It makes available a literary gem; a work of fiction that is ambitious, radical, innovative, clairvoyant, humorous in intent and execution, and wonderfully unusual.

NOTES

1. Respectively: Richard Messer, "Robert Myron Coates," *Biography*, vol. 102, *Dictionary of Literary Biography; American Short Story Writers, 1910–1945*, Second Series, ed. Bobby Ellen Kimbel (Detroit, Michigan: Gale Research Group, 1991), 43–47; B.D., "Notes on Novels," *New Republic*, September 18, 1929, 133; Benson, E. M., review of *The Eater of Darkness*, *New York Evening Post*, July 27, 1929, 6; John R. Clark, "Gaming in Modern Literature: Some Causes and Effects," *Modernist Studies—Literature and Culture, 1920–1940* 4 (1982): 151.

2. Malcolm Cowley, "Reconsideration," *New Republic*, November 30, 1974, 40.

3. Robert M. Coates, *The View from Here: Informal Recollections of Mostly Happy Yesterdays* (New York: Harcourt, Brace, 1960), 3–4.

4. *Ibid.*, 42.

5. *Ibid.*, 212–13.

6. W. G. Rogers, *Gertrude Stein is Gertrude Stein is Gertrude Stein: Her Life and Works* (New York: Thomas Y. Crowell Company, 1973), 110.

7. Robert M. Coates, Application for a Guggenheim Fellowship, 1928 (John Simon Guggenheim Memorial Foundation, New York).

8. Robert M. Coates, "Transition," *New Yorker*, November 12, 1955, 195.

9. Robert Sage, "Melodramadness," *transition* 4 (July 1927): 159.

10. Quoted in Hugh Ford, *Published in Paris: American and British Writers, Printers and Publishers in Paris, 1920–1939* (New York: MacMillan Publishing Inc., 1975), 76. Arthur Moss, "A Soft Note of Introduction" to *The Eater of Darkness*. Paris: Contact Edition, 1926, n.p.

The Eater
of Darkness

To
My Father and Mother
Nick Carter
"Sapper" (H. C. McNeille)
Elsa
Kathleen Cannell
Ex-Mayor Hylan
Gertrude Stein
Robert McAlmon
George Laflin Miller
Oleg Skrypitzine
J. C. Henneberger
Gerald Chapman
Harold Loeb
The New York Times
Jeannie Oliver Arnold, M.D.
I.B.F.
and
Fantômas
This book is affectionately
or gratefully dedicated

Iunctis viribus molestum contempsimus.[*ED1]

Petronius Arbiter.

CONTENTS

APOLOGUE

It seems it had been years but (she was remembering: a cold gray wind and the leaves went stuttering along the walls of the rue Clovis) it was hard keeping the cobblestones silent as into the rue Descartes; a man (waving a green pantaloon before the autobus) flattening into arm in arm.

"Et après ça Madame?" (reëchoing).

"Après ça il me faut une livre de carottes." (She fed herself into the vast conveyor belt of plate-glass windows blue signs with gold letters is the Place de la Contrescarpe (the expectant autobuses rustling with hooded plumage in the trees) and he had said)

"You must come and see me sometime": he had said:

"Will you come and see me sometime I will show you my studio the address is we will make tea together I shall give you tea": he had said:

"Come. You must come as to tea no matter but I shall cover you with the fragile petals of muguets and cigarette ashes so that your nudity may be scented and terrestrial by these means I shall drag you down from the stars placing violets on the nipples of your breasts roses and green vines in the (oh! Kiss-fertile) hollows of your knees I shall bring you within the compass of my arms": he had said and mentioning the number.

After that it had been easy and (she remembering) the rue Lacèpede the rue (feeling smotheringly the smooth slipping of silk along the cool flesh of her thighs) Gracieuse the rue du Puits-de-l'Ermite (remembering) walking:

◆

The concierge had had white hairy eyes very much like a photograph fading spottingly in the 1890 manner or still more closely resembling one of those wild thin figures seen walking after midnight above the Subway gratings on Seventh Avenue, and wielding her meager face like a broom:

"No. Monsieur Charles is not here any more."

(And (dropping like a penny in the slot machine French Girls Delight) between two men at the curbstone: she remembering)

"When will he be back?"

"God knows. He has gone to America."

The words tolled like a deathknell in her ear. Steadying herself with one hand against a large terracotta flowerpot which ornamented the square pillar at the foot of the stairs:

"Did he leave no word no address no message for me?"

"No," said the concierge. "You can," she [sic] added, intermittently rubbing a dustcloth against the face of a tall walnut clock, "go up and see if you desire. The studio is for rent."

She remembering opening the door and all floating glittering against the dusty air now:

(1) the tapestry from Yucatan it had hung over the fire-place,

(7) the tin garbage can in which he had kept his clay near the window,

(4) the square of Chinese silk; the (3) walnut table,

(5) the strip of muslin printed with marching kings she had once worn it as a sash dancing for him in a moment of abandon,

(6) the empty parrot's cage they had decorated it with watercolors together:

Tenantless days and the place was already haggard in rigor mortis: it needed sweeping: he had not even left the empty parrot's cage they had decorated in watercolors for her. Descending again to the concierge:

"I will take the studio. How much is it by the month?" she had said.

"Three hundred and fifty francs," said the concierge.

◆

She was (she was remembering) walking:

1—MONITORY FIGURES

We next find him in a rooming house. This rooming house was located on West Twenty-Third Street,[1] New York City, near the point where the street, changing from its air of frontier respectability, breaks into a slouching run for the Hoboken Ferry. The rooming house had a smooth brown front and brown worn steps which leaped into the entrance door like a rabbit into its hole. The house shivered clammily about you as you entered.

In the window nearest the doorway on the groundfloor was a small brass sign indicating the existence of the Seaside Employment Agency.

From the hallway, however, a door gave into what had anciently been the parlor of the house when it had been occupied by a doctor, or more probably by one of those families of the Eighties whose only outward show of life was when at ten sharp of every Sunday morning three ladies in bloomer-sleeved and wideskirted frocks descended the steps accompanied by a tall gentleman in frock coat and while gloves on their way to attend divine service at the Seventh Baptist Church. In this room, or parlor, the now chief ornaments were six highly

1. For reasons obvious to anyone familiar with the course of diplomatic events during the last half century, the street number cannot be revealed at this time.

glazed china canaries, arranged meticulously on the mantel of a pink marble non-practicable fireplace.

And since one, on inquiring for rooms, was ushered into this room, and since, sitting on one of the goldleaf chairs, one saw through the stiff lace curtains the blank back of the little brass sign heretofore alluded to, the exact location of the Seaside Employment Agency became, in the woolly moments of waiting for the entrance of the landlady, a matter for the keenest conjecture.

In fact the problem, and the possibilities of its solution attendant on such an act, were among the deciding factors moving Charles Dograr to engage a room there.

Two months and three days, however, had passed. He had progressed no whit nearer the solution of the mystery.

In the meantime, Charles Dograr lived in a little room on the top floor.

The room consisted of an aisle bluecarpeted between the bed and the wall of the next room which in all probability was similarly arranged and so across the front of the house. At the foot of the bed, this aisle was barricaded by a bureau or chest of drawers. Early in his occupancy, Charles Dograr had pushed this bureau or chest of drawers aside, so that he might get to his window with the view of opening it at night and closing it in the morning.

There was also a chair.

From the window, one could look across the street, where

a lady on the third floor had rigged a rope along the framework of the fire escape, on which she hung pink silk chemises alternately with blue.

Charles Dograr was quite content in his modest quarters.

In this room, then, for two months and four days, he had subsisted on graham crackers and a box of powdered milk, which he had bought in a delicatessen on Seventh Avenue as a reward to himself for having discovered that its name, when read backward, spelled 'milK.'

At three o'clock every afternoon, he read a chapter in Macaulay's "History of the English Nation." Often he lay abed all day, with his hands clasped beneath his chin on the pillow, while the chambermaid would come to the door and gaze at him bewilderedly.

He had only seven dollars in cash, and eighteen francs ninety centimes wrapped in a handkerchief. No one had told him about the want ads in the daily papers so he had no idea of how one went about getting a job.

Occasionally, also, he looked through the pages of a by now wellthumbed copy of *Cosmopolitan Magazine* he had picked up in Madison Square and speculated on the impregnability of the morals of the young actresses whose photographs were printed in the rotogravure section. Daily, upon rising, he thanked God heartily for having preserved him from the perils of his transatlantic voyage, and for His solicitous watchfulness during the first few days of residence in a strange land among strange people, whose ways were foreign to him.

But he enjoyed walking along Lexington Avenue, and from the fact that all the shopwindows along Broadway were brightly lighted, even though his promenades extended well past the hour of midnight, he drew a pleasurable thrill of fear.

Moreover, when the evenings bored him, he occupied himself with cutting out bits of paper into intricate designs. So, on the whole, he was quite happy, though a little apprehensive of the future.

2—THE X-RAY BULLET

One night, however, he was returning at five A.M. and his breast burdened with a longing for human companionship. The stairs mounting wearily ahead of him he paused at the third landing. A crack of light beneath a door had caught his eye and thinking to rest himself with a half hour of conversation he pushed open the door and walked in.

"Well, well, well, well, well, well, well," said the old gentleman as if he had been expecting him. "Sit in that chair."

Charles Dograr did as he had been directed. The old gentleman turned back to the table, or desk with marble top, at which he had been working. Charles Dograr observed that he had a remarkably white brow and long sinuous hands. He was naked, except that he wore a pair of long green silk stockings. His back was covered by a mass of tattooed inscriptions arranged in orderly rows and interspersed with formulæ and geometric designs like a page from a mathematical textbook.

Apparently these had bearing on the work in which he was engaged, for occasionally he would pause among his siphons, bunsen burners, retorts, hydrometers, test-tubes, Vernier scales, microscopes, aerometers, transformers, dynamometers, induction coils, crucibles to (with the aid of two small carved ivory handmirrors which he kept constantly at hand on the table before him) transcribe some one among the mass of notations and formulæ on his back.

The room was suffocated with the light from four hydrogen lamps in sockets on the ceiling. Over the head of the old gentleman Charles Dograr (thinking it at first an ocular illusion due to the superabundance of illumination) noticed a glittering sheet of light, curving umbrella-like downward as if some plane, otherwise invisible, refracted the rays of the powerful electrics. The room was still.

At the old gentleman's right, on the table, a black cloth shrouded some large and apparently intricate apparatus or machine.

Once, as he worked, the old gentleman pointed with a snakelike finger at his left leg.

"Table of logarithms," he said.

Charles Dograr cleared his throat. "Really?" he commented with vague politeness. "I live on the floor above, in the little—"

The old gentleman waved his hand impatiently. "Sh-h-h! Sh-h-h!" he whispered emphatically. "It's not yet time."

"I thought—" continued Charles Dograr, like a stone rolling downhill.

"Never mind," replied the old gentleman. "Wait!"

He was heating a test-tube over the flame. The liquid clouded, changed color, was green. The old gentleman chuckled. Someone snored in an adjoining room. Charles Dograr felt his mind slipping out of his body like a hand out of a glove. A pungent aroma invaded the air. The lights were hot. The old gentleman was pouring the contents of the test-tube into an orifice of the machine under the black cloth. He was tampering shrewdly with the lever of a stop valve as he did so, and watching the needle of a dial. He had lifted a corner of the black cloth, disclosing a spiderweb antenna strung between two blue-glass-rimmed apertures at the rear of a porcelain box and was busying himself with some thumbscrew adjustments.

Charles Dograr was lying back in his chair; his mind dazedly wandering; his nose, in the musk flavored air, the peaked roof of his soul.

How long he lay there he did not know. The night had been throbbing silently about him. Suddenly it was as if the room had been jerked up and down twice or thrice, but with such infinite rapidity that the motion had been imperceptible, save that a thrilled commotion remained in the air, leaving the room pulsing. He saw that the old gentleman had reached under the table and had pulled a lever.

The cloth had been stripped from the machine. It consisted of cogs, cams, levers, wires, coils, springs watchlike in delicacy converging in a tube, blued like a rifle barrel but not more than 2½ inches long and slightly flaring at the mouth. This tube was mounted on a swivel-joint controlled by a thumbscrew, making it susceptible of movement through an arc of approximately 135 degrees, and its movement was registered on a dial set in the base of the machine, where also a compass and incidence-meters made it possible accurately to orient the aim of the barrel. In general, the apparatus looked like a stereopticon gone berserk with machinery. Charles Dograr saw the ends of two electrodes, heavily insulated, in the box-like roof of the (as it appeared to be) incandescent-chamber. There were two other connections, sunk deep in Schiss-Mayer sockets, at the side of the contrivance. A jackknife switch lay open between them.

"Come now," said the old gentleman, as he folded the black cloth away. And, as Charles Dograr lay a moment, collecting his faculties, "Come on! It's ready."

Charles Dograr walked toward him. Midway through the room, he stumbled against something. Before he could regain his balance, he had swayed forward flinging out his hands, and had fallen heavily against a smooth, almost perpendicular surface, cold to the touch, *invisible* to the eye, which barred him off from the old gentleman whose bright eyes were watching him amusedly!

"That's my own invention!" he cried proudly, "The Dead Plane!"

Charles remained a moment, his spine prickly. He saw his hands, sustaining him against nothingness, saw the flesh at the side of his palms flattened under his weight against the chill invisible substance!

There was a crackling flare. The obstruction had been withdrawn. Considerably shaken, but oddly unafraid, he walked over to the side of the old gentleman.

The old gentleman looked at him slyly but cheerily. Within the Dead Plane, as the old gentleman had called it, the air was dull, and still. The earth is a great sleeper, and the heave of its deep-vaulted, slumbering belly sets everything on its surface to rocking in a rhythm so innate in us that we never, perhaps, perceive it. Suffice it to say that not until he had stepped inside the Dead Plane did Charles Dograr, looking at the chair on which the old gentleman sat, at the table at the machine upon it, understand fully the meaning of the term, "inanimate object."

These were still, motionless—but, gazing back through the microscope-slide phosphorescence of the Plane at the room he had just left, he saw (was it the shifted veiling of the Plane? Was it that here, from this suspended hub of silence, he saw the tremulous, eternal pulse of Life itself?) the furniture, the walls, the chair on which he had been sitting rippled over with the beat of an inward pulsation, vibrating like objects seen in a mirage.

As he stared, the Dead Plane glowed gradually visible, like a mist of ice, or rather as if a dense fog had been shaved in parabolic slices by a larger contrivance than those with which ham is cut in butcher shops. The outer room was vanishing behind an opalescent, translucent haze.

"I can close it down completely," chirped the old gentleman.

He moved a lever farther. A humming that had been faint became insistent. The Dead Plane clouded utterly, dense white opaque. The outer room was shut away. They were alone together in their cupola of silence, their faces glazed by the gray light of the interior of a submarine.

"Sit there. No. Put your eye to the left oculascope. That's right."

Rising V-shaped from a hooded housing at the base of the blue light-barrel were two tubes, ending each in an eyepiece lensed like the instruments of an optometrist. Charles Dograr seated himself at the left of the machine, his eye to one lens. The old gentleman, he observed, had taken his place at the other, and his hand grasped a lever.

"Look!"

He saw nothing. The eye of the lens stared at blackness. And then (in the corner of his eye he saw the hand move on the lever) it was as if he stared down the path of a searchlight, focussing [sic] an inch-wide disk of light on the clouded surface of the Plane.

It was an instant only. Then the disk had cut like an augur through the Plane, and the tiny circle of vision centred [sic] in blackness lay against the wall of the room. He saw a fragment of picture frame, a segment of wallpaper design.

Rodlike again it leaped beyond, his eye following. It touched the arm of a sleeper in the room beyond the wall—bedclothes—a giltbrass knob at the foot of the iron bedstead . . . it pierced the other wall—was boring the night-clad street—lay against the bricks of the house across the way . . . he saw blurringly. . . .

"Keep the focus. There, beside your eye-aperture."

He found the collar-swivel adjustment (as on field glasses) and the disk of sight leaped into clarity again. The old gentleman was increasing (by means of his lever) the (or what appeared to be, for Charles Dograr saw a pointer advance along a scale reading:

Yds. . . 10 . . 20 . . 30 . . (up to) . . 5000 beside the lever slot) focus or range of the contrivance.

Then he glued his eye to the aperture again.

Successively (as the range increased) he followed the x-ray bullet through the wall of the opposite house—a chandelier—plaster ceiling—beams—rafters. . . .

It impinged on the left nipple of the lady across the street, passed slantingly through the tissues, nerves, veins, arteries, bones of her body, issuing at a point slightly below the small of her back, whence (more rapidly as the old gentleman more eagerly extended the focus) it progressed swiftly through:

a bottle of glue
three eggs in a windowbox
a cigar
the mechanism of an alarm clock
the chain of an electric light fixture
four pages of the Graphic
the hand of the reader
an orange
an El station turnstile
a goldfish bowl
a cushion
the calf of Ann Pennington's leg
two kissing lips

an iron handrail
a corset string
a garbage can
a plate of ham sandwiches
Laurence Vail
a pack of cards
a glass eye
two felt slippers
the C in a Chop Suey sign
a cigarette holder
an umbrella
Reginald Marsh
a bottle of gin
an art-bronze book-rock
Theodore Dreiser
a clogged drain pipe
a sheaf of Shulte Cigar Store coupons
H. L. Mencken
a stiletto
Kenneth Burke
a stethoscope
a Martini cocktail
two pretzels
a cocktail shaker
Howard Young
Kathleen Millay
a pack of Luckies

Skeat's Etymological Dictionary
a copy of the New Yorker
a filing cabinet
seven picture post cards
a hot water bottle
a string of sausages
the handle of a frying pan
several bananas
as aspirin
a bottle of Zonite
a young girl
a pair of bedroom slippers
three shirts in a laundry bag
a bottle of ink
a dog's tail
a two-cent stamp
Mona Raille
a pajama button
the teeth of a man yawning
the left fender of a truck
a copy of Ranch Romances
a cup of coffee
a marble-topped table
a red necktie
a cross-town car
a taxicab
the tassel on a lady's garter

Malcolm Cowley
a tree
a street lamp in an open park. . . .[ED2]

"I call myself the 'Eater of Darkness,'" the old gentleman chuckled. The pointer was at 2250 yds. The x-ray rod of light had now launched on a long flight through darkness, save where once it flashed on and through the spars of a ship its pennant waving. They were traversing the Hudson.

"Look inside," commanded the old gentleman, opening a pinhole slot in the side of the machine. Charles looked— once—and drew back affrighted. He had never conceived such an inferno of cold incandescence. There had been no glare—if anything only a pale colorless glow. But it was as if a splinter of the sun had pierced his retina.

"I'll see if I can screw her up to 3000. She ought to stand it tonight."

Charles felt the old gentleman's hand crawling crablike along his leg as the lever advanced and the x-ray bullet bored on.

a pillar of the porch of a Colonial house
a brass doorknob
a hall stand
red velvet curtains
the transverse of a dim room
a Morris chair
a man's knee. . . .

"Ah! We've got something at last!"

The disk swung upward. A man's back—his vest button—a cigar—the nose—the socket of an eye. . . .

Two inches more, and Charles Dograr gazed at the inner vaultings of a living skull, at the dark and convoluted interior of the brain of that distant man!

The old gentleman leaned back and stared at Charles Dograr. Charles Dograr looked at the old gentleman and within his heart, he not knowing why nor whence it came, a sense of bitter and destructive mirth had seated itself and sat rocking his body with silent laughter.

"Let's read that," said the old gentleman. A moment later he dictated: "2,976 yards and about 2 feet." Charles noted down the figures.

"And now—see that switch?—between the two connections? Here are rubber gloves. When I saw: 'Now!'—CLOSE THE SWITCH!"

Their eyes went back to the oculascopes. A moment of fumbling, as the old gentleman adjusted the range. Then—

"Now!" cried the old gentleman. "Now! NOW!" in a voice like a mortar grinding pebbles.

Charles Dograr closed the switch.

Visibly, it was as if a snake of fire had wriggled out from the hooded orifice of the machine. Swift beyond sight, it had run down the thin and unswerving cylinder that marked the path of the x-ray bullet. The man's head—the brain Charles Dograr watched—jerked backward, as if the snake had struck

. . . it trembled a little . . . then fell slowly sidewise out of the disk of Charles' vision.

The old gentleman, unconcernedly, began to reverse the focus.

"I'm tired of practising on flies," he remarked.

Charles Dograr's breast deflated on his terror as on a ball of iron. One by one, the objects through which their gaze had passed reappeared for a moment (as the x-ray eye of the machine retraveiled [sic] its path) then vanished irretrievably in the night.

Charles (at last even the aperture in the Dead Plane closed; the x-ray bullet had re-entered its hooded home; they were alone in the cupped opacity of the Plane) watched dizzily. He knew what he had seen.

The old gentleman was consulting the compass. "West northwest by north, seven points," he read. Charles' hand moved lifelessly to his pencil and wrote it on the pad.

Now a set of maps appeared. One, labelled 'West Section,' the old gentleman quickly oriented. With calipers and rule he laid out the ("Read me that distance again."—"2976 yards and about two—" "All right, that's enough") course the x-ray bullet had travelled, marked where the serpent flash of lightning had struck, looked up smiling at Charles, whose eyes were shrunk fish-skins over his horrified soul.

But the old gentleman seemed to notice naught amiss in his young disciple's behavior; he was, in fact, cheerful rather than otherwise, to all seeming. "As I saw," he began without preamble, "I've quit practising on flies and such things. It is neither conclusive scientifically nor satisfactory personally. You're lucky, young man, that I brought you in here tonight. What did you think of it? You're calm enough. Good mettle underneath, I warrant that."

He had been talking at random, though his eye and manner were those of a man pursuing a hairthread point of logic. Now he suddenly produced a bottle and two tumblers, pouring a stinger for each glass. "Drink this. You can't be as steady as you look."

"No," said Charles, finding his voice suddenly weak as he spoke, "I . . . I'm not."

"Don't wonder," replied the old gentleman enthusiastically, as if the sudden collapse of Charles had been an unexpected admission of his contentions. "Struck you odd, eh? Reach out wherever we want, through darkness, bricks, wood, stone, metal, flesh—and then light a little invisible lamp at the end of our focus. Odd, eh? 'd I tell you? I call myself the Eater of Darkness. Good name. Call me that. You may not believe it, but the hardest job was to get the light-disk to cut darkness, and keep focus. Dust does it. Dust in the air. That's why I work at night, y'know. Too easy by day." A greasy leer was sliding like oil across his face. Charles felt the man's eyes move downward like fire, enveloping his body.

He felt he must speak. His words staggered.

"I called it the x-ray bullet," he ejaculated.

"X-ray bullet," the old gentleman repeated. "Good! Takes it all in." His hand pinched Charles' knee. "Clever. Clever lad. I like you."

"I can't get out of here," said Charles involuntarily, remembering the Dead Plane.

"No," said the old gentleman. There was a moment when the gaze of each settled immovably in the purpose of the other. Then the old gentleman turned to the bottle.

"Here," he suggested, "You'll need another shot before you go."

They drank together. Without glancing behind him, Charles knew that the Dead Plane had been withdrawn. He set down his glass.

"Now," he said, "I must go."

"Wait," said the old gentleman, then paused irresolute. Charles saw his thoughts flying like bats behind the old grinning face. "You'll need money," he brought out at last. Throwing open a drawer in the desk (or table) he pulled out a wad of bills and thrust it into Charles Dograr's hand. It did not seem odd to him to accept it.

"And now," concluded the old gentleman, "Watch the papers tomorrow for the account of what happened at 5:45 A.M. on Hillcrest Terrace, Union Hill. You and I know. But I want to see what the police make of it. Drop in for dinner tomorrow together. I'll show you where to get the finest *cotelette à la bretonne* on this side of the water. We'll do a little more"—he chuckled horribly—experimenting afterward!"

3—"EXTRA! EXTRA!"

He went to his room for a little while, and lay sleepless on his bed. Out of the darkness, like the face of a drowned man out of the sea, the house across the street was rising pale and expressionless.

It was near dawn.

The blanket crawled over him like a caterpillar.

He got up and went for a walk.

As the front door closed blackly behind him, a door opened simultaneously across the way, in the house where the lady lived. A blonde man carrying a derby hat issued therefrom and Charles Dograr, glancing up through the bars of the fire escape that had refracted so many of his ardent glances, thought he saw a white arm waved downward from the window.

The blonde man, however, did not look back. He walked off toward Tenth Avenue, carrying his derby in his hand like a man about to empty a cuspidor.

Charles moved in the opposite direction. There was a buttery tinge along the eastern sky. The streets were gray, the pavements relentlessly deserted. In the knife-edged early light the concrete sidewalk was like a skin stretched across the drumhead of Infinity. A too-loud step might provoke a premature alarm. Charles walked gingerly, like an incognito Paul Revere.

At Ninth Avenue the floating El dangled its spiderlegs

around him at Eighth Avenue a newspaper delivery truck spun past a man walked out of an allnight lunch at Seventh Avenue the houses were red along the dry street like shreds of meat on a bone at Sixth Avenue he turned north because there was a novelty store with gimcracks in its window and especially art photos of beautiful girls legally nude that he liked to look at.

Soon the first early groups of workers were moving in clumps along the sidewalk. He looked at their brutish faces and it gave him a sense, almost feminine, of fear.

There were so few of them.

For Charles Dograr was one of those rare souls whose spirit seems to have been compounded as it were, of more fragile substance, of emotion more volatile, perception more finely tunable than the rest, so that he rode currents of intuition that others sank through seeking the rock-bottom of logic, and was uplifted and exalted by the transcendental vapors of a perhaps earthy—even, to continue the figure ad locandum, miry—concept into which others, trudging, stuck bogged and bemisted.

So sound moved him more than hearing, vision more than sight, and his instinct sucked Truth, like honey, from the flower of Life, disdaining the syllogistic distillation of the comb. Briefly, he listened to the melody, not the words, of the Eternal Song, and he was just the person—perhaps the only one alive—to imagine there was any discoverable meaning in such a passage as this, when he found it in a book.

Thus he strode along, keeping as bold a front as he might, but inwardly wondering why one of these hawkeyed Italians did not knife him, or one of these thincheeked Jews garotte him with stiff brown fingers, or one of these thickjawed Bulgars bludgeon him—all for his pockets' contents as he walked alone among them (and they so few) between the empty-glass houses.

And one man followed him! It was a dirtyish little fellow, his clothes frizzled like a cocoon and a dusty derby hat. Charles turned down Twenty-Ninth Street. Iron shutters had been rolled down, closing the driveways of the warehouses. Overhead the sky had grown dark and thunderous.

"He's a head shorter than I" thought Charles. But Fear told him that little men could kill. Napoleon, Cyrus, Cæsar whirled through his head—all little men, but indomitable. . . . He pictured the man behind him—his steps were gaining; they were like thunder in the narrow way—he saw him a grayclad miniature thunderbolt, gritting his teeth, the hands clenched, the whole strung body tightening for the flashing destructive moment toward which it had been framed. "He will leap," thought Charles chokingly,—"from behind."

And he walked slowly, almost tottering—what did it matter? one step more or less away from his doom—and his hand slid falteringly along the slipping granite of the crowding buildings. "My money," thought Charles, "—the old gentleman; I have more than sixty dollars. . . ." And (vicariously) almost comforted—"What will he do with it? Sixty dollars. . . . Go to Chicago . . . drink . . . with sixty dollars . . ."

And then—the short sharp stab of revulsion. He sees his body lying there, lying in the gutter. Horses stumble over it.

The expressman leaping down from his seat. "Good God!" And the stenographers gathering round—screaming affectedly, for what is a dead body lying there in the gutter to them? They roll him over . . . "Stabbed!"

His heart sickened. A cold miasmal fluid rose within him, choking. Here he would wait. He would turn, bravely . . . meet death. And, pivotting [sic] funereally, he turned.

With a curious crouching carriage, the little man walked fuzzily past Charles and continued down Twenty-Ninth Street.

For a moment, Charles leaned unsteadily against a hydrant, staring, dumbfounded. Twenty or thirty paces farther on, the man came to a halt, fumbling in one of the pockets of his coat. Finally he produced a key, turned the lock of a door.

With a leap Charles was upon him. He touched the man's shoulder. The thin face turned blankly inquiringly up at him.

"What is your name?" he asked.

"Why, Rupert Pragman—Rupert C.—" began the little man in a voice like eating Grape Nuts. "Why?"

Charles felt that he could take him in his arms and weep with him. But he remained calm. There was a moment of silence.

"Is that all?" asked the little man, meekly, and began to sidle unobtrusively toward the door. Suddenly he stopped. "It isn't my wife?" he demanded, coming back with a little pounce to seize Charles' coat sleeve. "*It isn't my wife?*"

Charles shook him off. This was an untoward question; it upset him. "Do you love your wife?"

"Do I love . . . ? . . . Sure I . . . Say, what is it to you any- way? Who are you anyway?" He tried to put on a bold face but the eyes were like a child playing soldier. "Hey Charlie!" he shrieked suddenly toward the interior of the vacant building. "Don't think I'm alone here, you. What do you want anyway?" No Charlie came.

"I'm Charlie. Charles Dograr is my name."

Abruptly, the little man tried to manœuvre himself inside the door. Charles seized him, dragged him back. The man gave a half-choked squawk. Charles, until now, had preserved some semblance of calm. But at this, the floodgates burst.

"What's the matter with you anyway?" he cried, as dis- gust ripened into wrath. "Why didn't you kill me? You had me alone. I was waiting . . . counting every step. And not a soul around. Not one!" He dragged the fellow out of the doorway, twisted his head around. "Look! Look up the street—the other way too—not a soul in sight. Why didn't you? Why didn't you? Do you think I haven't got money? Why didn't you kill me?" He cuffed him about the head, slapping his face with the broad palm, raining questions like a schoolmaster on an offending pupil.

And—"*Good* Lord! *Good* Lord!" the little man was moaning breathless to himself struggling.

And Charles was near tears. "You . . . if you had the heart of a man . . . for your wife . . . with me all alone. . . . Listen!" He pulled him suddenly erect. "You say you love your wife. What would you do with sixty dollars?" The little man squirmed, voiceless.

Charles persisted. "What would you do? I've got it. You'd have it if you'd had guts enough. What would you do with it? Speak!"

"*Good* Lord!" cried the little man.

"Speak!"

"I–I don't know. . . . *Good Lord!*" Charles had wrenched his arm judiciously.

"How long do you have to work here for sixty dollars?" He had to crack him on the jaw before the fellow could answer.

"Two–two weeks."

"Two weeks! And in two minutes you'd have had it. What am I to you? Why shouldn't you kill me?" Charles' voice rose suddenly, jangled off human key. "God, man! Can't you speak? Can't you think? Faugh!" With a revulsion abrupt and brutal, he threw the man away from him. It was a reptile, a toad, a slimy thing to cover the hand that touched it with green scum. His hands would be foul for days. The little man scurried inside his glass door, locked it and remained inside, staring.

Charles walked to the curbstone and sat down and wept. "Humanity! Humanity!" he cried. "What is humanity that I should love it? . . . or fear it? . . . or pity it? . . . or—" this came more slowly "—hate it?"

That was judicial. "—Hate it. . . ." He turned. The little man, nose pressed to glass, gave a backward start but Charles smiled, as reassuringly as he might. Enunciating carefully, that the words might be seen though the door barred their sound, he said, "I forgive you," repeated it three times, smiled at the end, and walked away to the Pennsylvania station.

The morning papers were out, and he bought the *American*, the *World* and the *Tribune*, then went to the benches of the waiting room.

BOMB SLAYS TEN AS
THOUSANDS STARE

But this was in Roanoke, Va.

"I KILLED HIM," SOBS SON
CONFESSING DOUBLE CRIME

—obviously not that. Nor:

BRIDE SEES HUSBAND'S
FATAL PLUNGE

Though for a moment he had high hopes. But it had happened in Arcana, Ore. Hastily he turned to the second page, the third, the fourth. He found himself muttering, "Hillcrest Terrace. . . . Hillcrest Terrace, Union Hill. . . ." and checked himself sharply, glancing up to see if he had been observed. It was by such slips as this that the cleverest criminals were caught. From cover to cover of them all he went; there was no mention of his murder, so far.

"I'll wait for the evening papers," he decided and lay back comfortably a moment, lazily watching the tide of commuters, dozen by dozen, as they rushed pell-mell for the Subway.

They had a practised way, he observed, of dropping two cents and snatching a paper at the Union News stand as they passed. "Poor devils," he thought, "Too bad it isn't in the morning papers. Give them something to read."

◆

And again—he was sitting in a Thompson's Lunch, eating prunes and a doughnut off a chair arm—it came to him suddenly: "I am a murderer!"

"I am a murderer!" For a moment it seemed he had spoken it; for a moment he seemed to hear the echo of his voice rebounding from the tiled walls and he looked curiously at his neighbors—the man in brown the two sailors the man with the little black valise the truckman the plumber—eating silently. No one moved. The cashier sat behind his counter, face bent over the morning paper.

Perhaps one of these was a murderer was well. Perhaps the cashier had strangled his three-year-old daughter last night as the city lay sleeping. He had a face that curled round his blue eye like a fist around a marble. "He looks more like a murderer than I."

Charles Dograr hastily finished his doughnut. "This is unhealthy," he told himself, referring, of course, to his thoughts. "They all look more like murderers than I. But that little gray man. . . . Ugh! How looks do deceive one . . ."

"Eh? Oh! Yes, it does seem warm," and the cashier gave him his change.

Charles had stared. "I must stop talking aloud like that," he warned himself as he swung out into the Avenue.

"And I must stop thinking in that way. . . . But I did pull the switch. I did pull the switch."

◆

Windows, glittering magnetically, flaked the air like tangents of other spheres piled tier on tier above him marched converging before him. It was a crooning of motor axles coiling springlike outward along the stiff radial spoke to the oily such and slurrr, the rubber-and-asphaltum churn that grinds no corn and mills no grain but only the smooth cars flashing brass-and-glass-and-varnish-bright. Keen-snouted phalanxes routing the wind, their prey, down the Avenue; and Charles Dograr.

"Fed herself (himself likewise?" said he) "into the vast conveyorbelt of plate-glass windows blue signs. . . ." (as if out of a bubble remembering) the air piping clear; the street a spoke of the sun: but (he could not remember (except an empty gray-dusted room) and why? When? Where? Became the tall doorman in blue (blue signs? Blue signs?) handing the fat lady to her motor) an armored truck went by.

He recalled he had not slept: the inharmonious night pulling him almost physically backward with a drooping revulsion into (what? when? who?) some unremembered dream? Some unvisited locality? Had not some forgotten woman breathed the silver mail of her soul about him?

He was walking up Fifth Avenue: the pistoning men, aptly

moving, glozed with women as with oil.

They were all taking themselves so seriously. The moment past, Charles Dograr made himself serious. He swung his arms like the rest. He masked a face of "It's 4:37 now and I've got to be at the offices of the Hydraulic Compression and Resurfacing Company 999 West 48 Street at 11:30" over his whimpering soul. Resolutely he projected himself past the Astor Library.

He crawled down the blustering length of Third Avenue, passing, one by one, like an inch-worm on a yardstick, the calipering legs of the El. He turned a corner. Suddenly he remembered his sixty dollars.

He went into a drugstore and had a malted milk and a cream cheese sandwich. Then he went to Weber and Heilbroner's and bought six silk shirts ($4.40 each with two collars to match in the Manhattan Manner) light blue with white pin stripes really a charming effect very exclusive. Passing a five-and-ten-cent store he went in and bought several key rings, an egg beater, three can openers and a string of imitation pearls.

He had some vague idea of laying these, a votive offering, on the steps of the lady across the way. It must be remembered that he had not yet met Adeline. However, half an hour later, he had tossed all the bundles into a deserted garbage wagon on East Sixty-Third Street.

◆

It was dead time. Forty-Second Street bored him.

He went up to Columbus Circle and stared with yellow

eyes into the Park. He imagined himself a patient in Bellevue Hospital.

"What I really out to do," he said to himself, "is go to college."

A strange sense of peace swooped with white wings upon him—a solemnity causeless and absurd but lovely like white clouds in the sky—a peace that drifted, inwardly voluted, that lolled apart and drifted like clouds merging and separating again—and he stood silently on the street corner, wondering at the functions of the human body. He marveled that the man who lies down in a field of growing grain can ever arise again.

"Decomposition so intricately prolonged. A process of rot ingeniously subdivided and balanced against itself so that one part feeds on the decay of the other and man walks full seventy year. The vegetables are not vindictive," he said.

"Alive or dead," he told himself, "I am just so much manure. One hundred and sixty-five pounds of it, belong by right to the nearest field of corn. Take me out among the hills and lay me down there, a willing hostage from mankind, a tribute to the silent sway, the august overlordship of the Vegetable Kingdom.

"O mighty Milkweed, spare me now! Give ear, all succoring and all-powerful Potato, to my plea and stay Thy hand that I may speak.

"For we, Thy servants, too long have spurned Thee; Thy slaves, we have abjured Thee, flouting Thy high commands.

"And the spirit of Evil has grown strong within us, so that

we scorned Those that were merciful to us and despised Them
in whose mighty hands we are as dust.

"We have grown fat in the plenty Ye have afforded unto us;
in the time of plenty we have forgotten the bitterness of Thy
wrath, too long withheld. And a darkness has fallen upon our
souls; and the puny power within us vaunteth itself.

"With the empty air are our bodies puffed up. Yea, even
with the empty air have we swelled up our souls, so that we
cried for all Earth to hear that we are Earth's masters.

"And we have turned to the Heavens, the Unknown and
Unknowable. 'Look up!' we cried in our boasting. 'Look up to
Heaven. There find ye light!' forgetting that inward Light Ye
gave us, warming our bellies, and threading our veins with life.

"We have turned from the Known to the Unknowable:
we have taken the Unassimilable for the Assimilable. And our
bodies are broken; and our spirits cast down. And of right shall
Thy bitterness fall upon us; of right shall Thy wrath be loosed.

"But here cometh one who shall be Thy bondsman always.
In all ways shall his spirit follow Thee; and his body gladly will
he sacrifice unto Thee, that his body may be Thy body, and his
soul Thy soul.

"Let his heart lie among the roots of the Elm-Tree, that his
soul may rise among Its branches.

"Let his loins lie among the roots of the Green Corn, and
his reins among the roots of the Gooseberry Bush, that his soul
may flower and give fruit with Them.

"Let the flesh of his legs lie among the roots of the Tomato
Vine, that his soul may prosper with Them.

"Let the flesh of his arms lie among the roots of the Wheat-Stalk; and his brain lie among the roots of the Mountain Laurel; and the flesh of his thighs among the roots of the Fir-Tree; and the bones of his body among the roots of the Green Grass, that his soul may live and flourish with Them, through all Eternity.

"Here cometh one among you, proclaiming you King, that his soul may be assoiled.

Amen. Amen. Amen"

And he added: "*En ceste foy je vueil vivre et mourir.*"

At that moment a man with a washable necktie and a brown suit bumped against him. There was a swimming moment and buildings rocking. Charles slammed into him with both fists. Fifteen or twenty passers-by paused. Charles turned to them.

"This man would drag down the Fair Name of American Womanhood into the Mire of Infamy," he proclaimed, pointing to his recumbent antagonist. "Bearing the outward semblance of Honor, Uprightness, and the Spirit of Fair-Play that is typical of American Manhood, he worms his way into the sanctity of the American Home, and there works his foul way unobserved. That man—," he drew himself to his full height— "was trying to get my wife to run away with him. And besides, he's a Bolshevist!"

A confused murmur rose from the hoarse throats of the crowd—a mingling of cheers for Charles, and threats for the unconscious victim. Charles with charming modesty, raised a deprecative hand and vanished in the direction of the Grand Central.

The afternoon editions were out. Hot from the presses, they had the results of the first two races at the Belmont Track, the Giants-Red Sox score through the fourth inning, and a telephotograph, rather blurred, of a wreck on the Santa Fe, near Baker, Idaho.

This much of the front page. Charles took a copy of the *Journal* and walked to a seat in the men's waiting room. He felt he must sit down. He had an odd feeling, as if he had drunk too much water. The room was humming like Judgement Day and spurting with light and

JERSEY MAN SLAIN BY UNSEEN HAND

———

Falls By Murder Bolt As Friend Looks On

———

New Killing Baffles Police Seek Morning Mystery-Visitor

Early this morning, as he sat in the library of his home at 133 Hillcrest Terrace, Union Hill, with James Larton, his lifelong friend and fellow-astronomer, Death struck to the brain of Edward B. Trulge, retired business man, member of one of New Jersey's oldest families and amateur student of astronomy, leaving him lifeless.

It was not the bullet, not the knife that cut him down. It was a weapon invisible as the wind, swift as the lightning, incredible as a fairy tale come true. Edward Trulge is the first victim of a method of murder which, if the prognostics of Captain

"Well, I suppose it's
        not so important
    beside the affairs of a
    nation but they gave
        a lot of space to
    "Is it possible? A
    whole column!" A
                tinkle of
    exultation
        falling
            in an ice box
    he felt sweat
            cold-white his
    face tangibly like glue to
    his gums and his nose it
    was cutting his brain "It
    is cutting my brain! My

M. R. Stope, Chief of the Union Hill Police, called hurriedly to the scene, are true, marks the beginning of a carnival of crime unparalleled in the history of the world.

Edward Trulge was electrocuted by an electric discharge coming no one knows how from no one knows where. The whole interior of his skull was literally cooked like the contents of a crucible, set in an electric furnace. According to the opi

far as can at

Lacking more

5000 degrees cen

  As h

finrst face clapped

          a blue black mark on his
          only   certain a man
        has le   he secret of
the lightning   d   dcontrit at
   no ot ay   hanwe expn
  When the surg   scalped
revealed the interi   of theddnd
burned to a cris   Comwhe
estim   at   onfas   enou
core of a   stricke
ssioner Ho   GOD!   with no
known forc   ve one
ere someh   elive   fiend in
can contr   power   for evil
  hellish   hearconveiceert
    eert cannoavenafter
    I willing
      o enemies
      timevebeena

Fire

face like oil

white   they   must

see!" he was clinging to

the paper as to the gun-

wale of a ship. His intes-

tines a cold

"So this is it! So this

is it!" He set himself

doggedly to endure.

God!

was glutting his intestines; wrapped coldly his throat in a pulsing hand and "I must get out" stupidly conceived the floor to be walkable. Somewhere back of his thought the room made a switching turn and there were suddenly great bulging noises his heels drumming his ears and faces ballooning upward horrifiedly he made a sickening attempt to wave his hand and for a moment the ceiling collapsed upward, fringing.

He was lying flat on his back. His hand hurt and his head hurt. He seemed to remember having seen a naked old man in a bathtub and a man bent above him.

"Are you Cousin Herbert? I'm Foster."

The man was evidently very excited and quite pale and it seemed to Charles unnecessarily fussy.

"I don't know how I'd have found you if I hadn't been right here when you fell and seen you reading the paper. Isn't it terrible? We should have told you more in the telegram. Such a shock! Such a shock! Here, can't you help me lift him up to a seat instead of standing around there? Easy, now. He's just had a terrible shock.

"Now," he suddenly sat down and Charles felt little brown eyes like lead pencils leaving marks all over him. "Can you walk? Can you get to a taxi?"

Charles felt his brain within his unobedient body gnawing like a ferret at the man's words.

"So you're Cousin Foster?" he ventured.

"Yes. And we thought I'd meet you at the train to break it to you. But I must have missed you. And then I walked through the station and just by good fortune I was passing. God! Such a shock! And can you imagine us this morning when they told us what had happened to him? For a moment when I saw you fall with the paper in your hand I thought you were another one. Here! Taxi!"

And inexplicably, standing in front of Ligett's Drugstore, on that busy corner, he began to weep, his cheeks wrinkling up into little furrows.

"I came on the 9:35," Charles ventured, analytically.

"Oh! Yes, yes! Terrible! Terrible!" he blubbered while the taxi driver stared in amazement.

"The first train I could get," Charles hardly knew what to do. He couldn't cry with him. He put his arm around his shoulder. "Every one is terribly upset. Cheer up. Cheer up."

The driver was leaning around in his seat to catch the address. "Where to?"

Charles waited. Now he'd find out. "Where to?"

Foster glanced at Charles and then blurted, "Union Hill. 133 Hillcrest Terrace."

Seated side by side with the son of his victim, Charles Dograr was riding to the home of the murdered man!

4—FROM A SCOTLAND YARD DOCKET

The most diligent search in all directions by a trained body of experts has been comparatively barren of information as to the past of the singular old gentleman with whom, at the lodging house of West Twenty-Third Street, New York, Charles Dograr began his curious adventure.

"At the time of which we write, he was known in the lodging house above referred to as Mr. Constantin. To the curious he gave out that he was a retired professor of chemistry from a Western university. He admitted to a hobby for photography. There is ground for belief that he was born in Bâle, Switzerland, of an upper-class bourgeois family. His father was a dealer in curios and old books. He was educated in Laussanne. Upon leaving there, he spent six years at Oxford, specializing in the Eastern languages. His career at the English university was unmarked by any irregularity.

"That, at some stage of his career, he had kept many a lonely vigil beside the heavy-shouldered, the ruffian sea, the ruffed and petticoated, creaming sea, its void immensity (perhaps in the quality of a Life Guard on the New England coast whose rocks rise stark from the billows) no one who has ever looked into his hawk-hooded eyes can doubt. At what time this was, however, one can only conjecture. After his death (the spectacular details of which, as will be recorded later in these pages, were given perhaps undue prominence in the newspapers not only of New York but of all the other large American cities as well) a certain Mrs. Aht of Erie, Pa., laid claim to his estate, alleging that, after living with her as man and wife during seven years, he had deserted her and their two children in June, 1908. She described his profession as that of a stone mason.

"He was recognized, though disguised as a bishop, at the Polo Grounds, New York, by Operative B639, who had had occasion to know him in India during the Hillfield uprisings, of which he was supposed to have been the moving cause. Simultaneously with his residence on West Twenty-Third Street (and his participation in the singular events the recital of which make up the body of this chronicle) a certain Thorn-dyke Smithers was holding open house in one of Long Island's most palatial residences.

"His apparent profession was that of a stock broker. He was daring behind the hounds; despite his advanced age, he was noted for his recklessness on the polo field. He drank deep and hearty. By these traits, as well as by the unprecedented magnificence of an unending series of fêtes and festivals given on the lawns or in the halls of his mansion, this Thorndyke Smithers had attained to undoubted leadership in the faster set of suburban society. He was none other than the old gentleman with whom we have affair.

"A curious type in the annals of criminology! In a letter to a friend in Kratensberg, dated from Bellow's Falls, Vermont, and found among his effects after his death, the following unusual phrase appears: 'God knows, if ever a gutta-percha soul resided in an India-rubber body, that man is I.' This is especially curious in that the reverse would seem to be true. He was always intriguing. An acquaintance states that he once saw the old gentleman, opening a borrowed book, find a visiting card, left as a place-marker, between the leaves. The name printed thereon was: M. Carlos Becerra. Upon observing it, the old gentleman fell into a revery lasting a full half hour, from which he roused himself to favor the acquaintance there present with a long and exceedingly learned disquisition on the waning ideals of human greatness. Upon the friend's observing, 'Egad, Tom, I'd no idea you were a classical scholar!' the old gentleman responded pithily and, as it turned out, significantly, 'The classics, if not the butter, are certainly the bread of my daily life.'

"Meantime, the residents of exclusive Thirty-Eighth Street had occasion to smile at the harmless eccentricities of the aged inhabitant of a dark old house near the corner of Madison Avenue. He wore shell-rimmed spectacles, wheeled himself about in a bathtub-shaped, rubber-tired contrivance and received no one though truckloads of canned pears arrived daily at the back entrance. He passed his days sitting at an upper-story window, tearing up bits of paper and throwing them into the street with inconceivable rapidity, and in such quantities that on some afternoons the tiny particles lay to a depth of three inches on the sidewalk before the house and traffic through the street was seriously impeded. Again, it was the old gentleman. In this identity, he posed as M. Carolo Faudras, Ex-Ambassador to Sweden, though what nation he had represented was never revealed.

"He had a habit of wiping his left eyebrow with his right forefinger. This gesture became almost frenzied at the crisis of the cytherean moment. It was by this fact that he was recognized by Fraülein Netta Felder, the singer, in Sofia, during the Fall of 1906. He had also a liking amounting almost to an obsession for Washington pie.

"After the downfall of the Crime Ring in New York, of which he was the acknowledged head, trunk lines capable of carrying a current of 700,000 amperes were discovered, leading to all of his various residences from the power-houses of the Addington Power and Light Company, Flushing, Long Island. For what purpose these were designed is not known but the directors of the Addington Co. were indicted and held as accessories before the fact in his crimes. The trial is still pending.

"Two photographs of him, as far as is known, are alone extant. One, taken at about the age of twenty-five, shows him, in white serge and a yachting cap, promenading before the Café de Paris, at Cannes. The other, taken perhaps fifteen years later, shows him as one of the ensemble taken of the participants in a fancy dress ball, where and exactly when not known. He wears the costume of a Hindu Rajah, with turban, fisbah, pantaloons and ceremonial sword thrust in a jeweled sash. He stands behind and a little apart from the rest, with his arm thrown over the shoulder of a naked model.

"He was tried: in Paris, August 1895, for arson and manslaughter; Vienna, March 1899, attempted rape; Chicago, October 1904, shoplifting and barratry; Edgewater, Illinois, in 1904, drunkenness, obscene language and resisting arrest; El

Paso, Texas, January 1907, conducting a game of chance; St. Petersburg, July 1911, attempting to cash non-valid checks; at Brussels, August 1911, complicity in the attempt to rob the Burgenhause Bank; Lyon, France, September 1919, forging identification papers; Calcutta, July 1921, running a house of prostitution without a license. In each case he received a verdict of acquittal. . . ."

So much and no more shall we quote from the Scotland Yard Docket. Little as it is, and small an insight as it affords into the man's character, it is all that the greatest detective organization in the world could discover about the strange man— Benjamin Constantin, Thorndyke Smithers, Prince Eugène de Montenegro, Carolo Faudras, E. Burke, Wynn Holcomb, René Fonstant, Edouard Percy, Aaron Glemby, Comte de la Birette, Thomas Malling or Thomas Wallace—call him what you will—who now sits in the room on Twenty-Third Street, methodically planning the greatest coup of his career!

5—"YOU ARE NOT COUSIN HERBERT!"

But first (and in New York Charles Dograr riding) the Seine behind the gleaming bridges was a long blue laugh through the painted lattices of a window (blue blue-green green-yellow but a scum of scarlet filtering the trees) purple-blue blue-green (beneath the red strake of a (for a (yes) moment the blue the) barge plugs the yawning bridge and a woman in a black petticoat: she stacks a dumpy figure against the thrust of a tiller: and then (oddly) life is empty again all empty and:

Thought, action, the drifting inconsequent activities of men women horticulturally repeopling the streets men women drifting (even the vociferous buildings (gray-blue) the sirening spire of Sainte Chapelle drifting) a moment and:

Lolling fading into the vacuous wide inviting smile green blue-green gray-blue of the (yes) Seine was a scimitar; the dark air curved beneath its destructive blade but:

Hastily she remembered the chocolates not that life matters but:

She turned away but:

It cannot be said that Charles Dograr had the faintest perception or apperception of all this. Not the distance that separated them (Paris from New York is approximately 4,377 miles, plotted on the slum-sline); not the difference, real or apparent, in location and situation between the two can be urged in explanation or mitigation of the fact. For, unquestionably, the lady who walked the bridges of the Seine and looked down into its lucent waters and thought of the drifting lives of men and women and started back at last from the horror of suicide—that woman was thinking of Charles Dograr.

But for Charles Dograr, riding in the taxi with Francis the son of Edward Trulge, it was only as if one segment of his brain were rapt in a dream his grosser senses could but hint at—in a flash of wheels axles turning thin horns piping (against the Macy's sign)—in an unrememberable glimpse of blue fading and deepening to purple and netted dripping in scarlet (into the screech along the rotted shoring as the ferry nosed bluntly into its slip).

Reader, have you ever felt (the stiffthroated buildings, the ironcoursing streets fading before your eyes) that you were but the semblance of another's dream? Has it seemed (your vision bursting for a moment into keen nothingness) that you were but the lymph in the organs of some gigantic creature's being, your whole life but a gesture of that organism's functioning? Has it come to you, sometimes, to have been swept by the breath of a woman's passing—some unknown woman, perhaps, who had come to you in dreams but with face always averted and now (for a moment) you are caught in the golden tissue of her hair, you are filled with a rich and elusive perfume—for a moment only, and she passes unseen unheard, and you are whirling again in the spate of the crowd?

So Charles Dograr. He thought it was God. He was wrong.

But he left it all, unheeding, in one small bubbling corner of his brain. Moments were precious now.

Discreetly questioning Cousin Francis, [sic. should be Foster] he had learned:

1. Cousin Herbert (ex tem. Charles Dograr) lived in Bridgeport, Conn. He had two aunts, Mary and Louise.

2. Uncle Edward, (the murdered man) always wore blue socks.

3. Cousin Herbert studied architecture. He had a dog named Shep.

4. His name was Herbert Trask. He had been a favorite with Uncle Edward because both had a weakness for astronomy.

5. He (Herbert) had not visited Union Hill for seven years. He would be surprised how it had grown up.

6. Adeline had been in Bridgeport last summer to visit Herbert's mother.

7. Old Mr. Carroll drank as much as ever.

8. Adeline was Adeline Laggick. She was also a niece of Trulge, but on the mother's side.

9. Mr. Larton had left the Repeater Coin-Filling Company and was now with the Spencer Eye-Dropper Corp.

Things fringed. Herbert had apparently once lived (10) on a farm, because Francis talked of the summer he had spent visiting them, when they had jumped into the pigpen and tried to play toreador with the sow.

"Of course. Of course," assented Charles. "Lord, how long ago that seems, though. How many years was it, anyway?" seeking verification.

But Francis was of that curious type who have so solemn a concept of Time that they lapse into an awed silence whenever

a date or term of years is mentioned. Now he went into a kind
of cogitative trance, pointing his eyes down his nose.

"Why, let's see—it was four years ago when we went up
to Worcester and I remember Aunt May saying at the time
that . . ." (Stick to Uncle Edward's blue socks and (Out of the
debris of information he had received Charles was beginning to
construct a kind of trestlebridge across the abyss of danger that
confronted him and) "How is Aunt Mary? Doing well?" . . . and
he would be back at night to the old gentleman with a grand
tale to tell. But—sucking like a sponge at his stomach as his
mind span to a thin bright disk—was this girl Adeline! A dark-
faced sallow-haired girl (so he saw her) sitting in a Morris chair
and apparently she had seen the real Herbert last summer in
Bridgeport. She leaps to her feet as he enters the door, points
an accusing finger. . . . (In the meantime they were climbing
a long hill above railroad yards. A river. . . .) What to do with
Adeline? . . .) ". . . and yet it couldn't have been 1910 because I
. . . West Virginia so I suppose . . . I swear, Herbert, you've got
me all mixed up. It seems it must have been 1909, but if . . ."

"1907!" Charles dumped out of his mouth like a piece of
indigestible pudding. Francis took it up and chewed it. "Let's
see. I'd have been seven years old. That don't seem . . ."

And then the brass doorknob! The Colonial porch! Inside,
there would be red curtains. . . .

The brass doorknob swung in. There were red curtains.
A long hall. Charles was sure he had uttered a slight cry. He
found himself shaking hands with a B-shaped lady dressed in
black. "Aunt Louise, this is Herbert. I found him in the Grand

Central. He fainted. Say, Aunt Louise, when did we go up to Hawk Center to see Herbert? 1909?"

"How is Aunt Mary? Doing Well?" asked Charles mechanically, in a faint voice.

The wallpaper was the most vivid thing in the room where they had ushered him. At regular intervals across an expanse of cottony carpet the furniture erected itself, like tombstones in a churchyard, with an air of gloomy but indomitable insistence. All the rest of the family were drawn up to receive him in a bay window around a fern standing in a hammered brass tabouret. It gave the impression that every other room in the ponderous and moldering house was empty.

All sensation of pity or of repugnance vanished from Charles' heart.

"This is Mr. Constable. I don't think you ever met him but you must have heard Edward—poor . . . ("Dear Edward I can't imagine . . . ("Oh! If the police would only . . . ("Now now you know that Mr. Larton . . . (An as yet unidentified lady in a checked taffeta blouse burst into violent tears and Charles riveting) . . . said that they are nothing more than a pack of . . .") . . . do something about . . .") . . . how any one could have . . .") . . . dear Edward he spoke of him often." Charles did not hear.

His attention had been caught by a series of rhythmic and resounding thumps that appeared to emanate, through the ceiling of the room, from the floor above. A vague premonition prompted him to speak.

"Where is Cousin Adeline?" he asked. At this moment, the thumping stopped. Every one appeared disconcerted.

"We must get him some tea," remarked Aunt Janet, as if she had been nudged from behind.

"I *said* somebody ought to get poor Herbert some food. I *told* you when I came in how he fainted in the railway station."

"Where is Cousin Adeline?" he had asked.

"Louise, won't you go out and see if there isn't some of that nice veal pie left?"

Obscuring more and more of the vine-and-bird-and-flower wallpaper in geometric ratio as his form advanced, Mr. Constable set himself in motion toward our hero. There was something reminiscent of the blanket held before a bull in his manner and Charles sensed suddenly that by his question he had in some way frightened them, and that to Mr. Constable's board-of-director's-meeting manner had been left the explication by the rest.

"You have often, doubtless, heard, Cousin—may I, too, share the honor of relationship—though only temporarily—in the Trulge family at this moment of affliction?—Cousin Herbert, in I am sure your wide acquaintance with the literature, not only of this day, but of other generations and other ages, the story of the clown, the clown who bleeds as he laughs, smiles as he weeps? Pagliacci—the grandest, to my mind of Puccini's operatic compositions—is the most famous example of the timeworn situation—so timeworn, in fact, that we are apt, in hastily condemning it as trite, to lose all sight of the fundamental truth . . ."

Charles, with his nose for paradox, could not help here sniffing a new trail.

"A truth, too often repeated, becomes by the fact, untrue: you wish to say?" he queried.—"I must interrupt to thank you for leading my mind to the consideration of the curious phenomenon. Though until this moment it had escaped my attention it is, on the face of things at least, an indisputable verity.

"In Art, of course . . ." he went on, meditatively. "Truth, decreasing in its enunciation; it is an awesome thought. And in life . . . Truth, a mental suit of clothes, to be outgrown—or, as you put it, outworn. Truth—the distillate of needs, desires, customs themselves transitory, building on the Truths they have brought forth. Truth—the milk of the cow, if the cow itself fed on that milk. Truth—the coral island, if the polyps themselves inhabited it." He seized Mr. Constable's amazed hand.

"It is, sir, a holy thought. The Well of Truth! . . . Of course. How wise, sir, were the ancients! A well runs dry with too much drinking.

"And one can continue," he continued. "Truth, like all things else, fatigues itself in repetition. The secret of revolution. One verges, perhaps unwisely but as always with new systems, on an attempt to define the motivation of all human progress. The truth of mortal ethics—a carpenter's rule, measuring the path to Eternity. The carpenter, Man, marks the edge with his finger, and advances the ruler another length. . . ."

"Exactly. Exactly," Mr. Constable cut in, and Charles saw the man had entirely missed the point. "One cannot too often confirm a thing that is true. And here, as it happens,—in this house, we have an example. For at this moment—if at this hallowed time I may use a profane illustration—we find our-selves, so to speak, backstage, at the moment when Pagliacci, in this case a feminine one, must distill laughter from her tears.

"The loved one is dead; the family cluster about the death-bed. . . . Pagliacci's heart is breaking. . . . But the call sounds. The curtain is rising. The audience must be amused. The audi-ence . . . must be . . ." It appeared for a moment that Mr. Con-stable would be carried away in the sweep of his own emotions.

But he regained his voice and continued. "So Adeline—brave girl. No one, we all know, loved her Uncle more deeply, more truly than she. No one, we know as well, will more eter-nally perpetuate his memory in the shrine of a devoted heart. And yet—"

Aunt Janet suddenly thrust her face between them. "But folks might talk, y'know, if they knew. She's got to go on, though I always did say that a profession that the Church frowns on—"

The heavy tones of Mr. Constable steamrollered her out of existence. "Exactly. Exactly. We who know her will venerate her fortitude the more highly. But the outsider, who might not know . . ."

Charles was utterly at sea.

At this moment, through the double door of the hallway, entered a girl—*the* girl, the beauty his soul, unknowing, had dreamed of. She was tall, long-limbed, smooth-moving. Her eyes were black, and sparkling. Caught negligently over the curve of one shoulder a silken scarlet cloak floated out in the speed of her graceful advance.

The other shoulder was bare. Bare, too, the firmly-mod-elled, branching slope from the creamy-columned throat downward to where a bandage of gilt cloth, woven with sil-ver spangles, just confined the tender-pointed breasts. Thence downward, the pink-tinted, delectable torso was cobwebbed o'er with a veil of gossamer gauze (and the recreant orb of Charles caught unashamed in the network of imitation pearls sewn shimmering thereon) which fell, diaphanous and disar-rayed, until a similarly-spangled gilt loincloth confined its way-ward folds more closely about her marbled lower limbs.

"Adeline!" gasped an aunt.

"Tea?" cried she, uncomprehending.

Mr. Constable retained his grasp of the situation. "I have just," he began tactfully, "been telling Cousin Herbert of the inspiring similitude between the tale of Pagliacci and your devotion, in the face of your dear Uncle's demise, to your Ori-ental dances."

Her eye turned in Charles' direction, and a flush, deli-ciously delicate, mantled her glowing cheek. For a moment their eyes met, and a buzz of ardor leaped in his.

"Why—but—but—he is—why—" and then, searing, direct—"*You are not Cousin Herbert!*"

He leaped the window, sped across the lawn. Down the street to the corner—a passing trolley—a burst of speed. . . . Charles scrambled aboard, but even as his nickle [sic] tin-kled in the farebox, so a thought dropped ringing in his heart. Her tone—the words still sounded in his ears, the intonation would linger with him always—had there not, yes, had there not been a tinge of joy, like roselight across the eastern sky at dawning—a cadence in her voice as of Love surprised and palpitating?

6—BARED FANGS

B ut my dear," questioned Mrs. Taitch, "Are you not afraid?" The two ladies are sitting over late tea, on the enclosed side-porch of the Pragman home in Yonkers. There are purple hills in the background, and the sun glows like magenta moonlight, with shadows reclining, chill, violet and still, behind the Dutch-cut trees that cluster in black-outlined groups among the deep-napped verdure. Far down the undulating valley-side, smoke rises from the chimney of a solitary farmhouse, stenciling fleetingly across the sunset clouds: "But Best's Coal—It's Best!"

"Don't be silly!" laughed Mrs. Pragman. But her voice trails golden into the silence that tottered, dense and precarious, over their heads. She had been talking at random, to gain time. Now, she raises her eyes and a silver wire of premonition tautens along the fused glances of the two women.

"I wonder," Mrs. Pragman wondered, "I wonder . . . my husband . . . can anything be . . .?"

It was, as it happened, exactly 3:35 P.M.

◆

At 3:36, Mr. Randolph Flock, living at 842 East 75 St., coined the phrase: "You may have a barrel of moment, but you look like a hogshead to me," which later won the $10,000 Slanguage [sic] Prize offered by the Daily News.

◆

At 3:37 a taxi turned the corner of Rivington Street into Allen. Midway in the block, a man stepped out of a real estate office. In the taxi, a man sitting beside the chauffeur turned to three men sitting in the tonneau.

"That's him! That's him!" he called excitedly. "Let him have it."

One gun jammed. The other two fired almost simultaneously. Hit, the man on the sidewalk hurled himself toward the hallway.

"Give him the works, the bastard! Let him have it. Get him!"

A woman sitting in the apartment house doorway rose, leaned against the carved ornamental stone pilaster and collapsed. A stain widened hastily on the back of her cheap blouse. From within the hallway, the shot man was firing automatically. The cab took up speed, dodged a truck around the corner and toward the river.

◆

In the third car of a downtown express, waiting above the 96th Street station for a Bronx Express to clear, Lucius M. Pilbore looked at his watch. 3:38.

◆

At 3:39 the famous producer of the Vanmore Follies—Karyl Vanmore—finished telling the latest one to a group of friends sitting in the dark pit of a theater. He turned toward the stage, gummy with girls in tights, rompers, knickers and bathing suits.

"Let's see the big ones," he called.

A man in shirt sleeves and a checked cap, standing on the stage was herding a file of mediums to the wings.

"Now stand here and keep together," he admonished them pettishly. "And you ones that Mr. Vanmore wanted to speak to later keep to this side. . . . Now the show-girls. All the show girls out here, please. . . . Hurry up now, d'you want us to send y'aninvitation?" A subdued titter ran among the girls.

Gradually a line of statuesque creatures formed along the footlights.

"Nobody that don't want to leave New York," counselled Mr. Vanmore. "Nobody that don't want to leave New York, Chapin."

"Nobody that don't want to leave New York," repeated Chapin. Two or three dropped out haughtily at this announcement.

Mr. Vanmore, standing with hands behind his back at the foot of the aisle, glanced along the row of faces. "Why, hello, Amy. . . . Back again, Melissa. . . . Here's Teddy, too. . . . All the old familiar faces. . . . How are you, Snoots?"

"Just fine, Mr. Vanmore," the girl's voice sounded ludicrously feeble in the empty theater. All the others were nodding and simpering.

"All right." He was suddenly and—as is the privilege of a famous producer—untransitionally brusk. "Let's have some music." A tinny piano in the wings struck up a waltz. "Well, now, girls. Walk. Keep time. . . ." They started in a slow prancing circle. . . . "A little slower Chapin."

"A little slower, Jerry," Chapin relayed it to the piano man.

◆

At 3.40 [sic] the dumbwaiter bell rang in an apartment on West 119 Street. Mrs. Flakkan answered the call by opening the dumbwaiter door.

"Meat ma-a-an," came the call up the stale-flavored shaft.

"Send it up," she called back. "It should 'a been here a half hour ago."

◆

At 3:41, Charles Dograr opened the door of Room 407 L. H. Sykes & Co, Hotel Agency, in a building West Twenty-Ninth Street and walked up to the girl at the switchboard.

"May I speak to Mr. Rupert Pragman?" he asked politely. "It's very important."

"Pragman? Pragman? . . . Yasure itain Boardman?" the girl asked. "There don nobody uh thaname woik here."

"No, it's Pragman."

"Well, there donobody name Pragman woik here."

He went out to the corridor. It was the seventh office he

had tried. But the man must work somewhere in the building.

Room 409
ART-TEX Kraft Rugs
J. R. Kennedy, N. Y. Mgr.

He opened the door. A fat man sitting behind coils of cigar smoke glanced up at him inquiringly. The window was grimy.

"Is there a Mr. Rupert Pragman working in this office?"

The man moved his head slowly from side to side, then turned his gaze toward a large illustrated calendar on the wall.

"Thank you," said Charles Dograr, and went out.

Room 411
Buckeye Belt and Leather Corpn.
F. S. Knox, Prest.

A girl peered out from beneath a sign Information.

"May I see Mr. Pragman—Rupert Pragman?"

"Pragman . . . he's in Shipping, isnee?"

"I—I think so," agreed Charles affably.

The girl had her lips to the phone and was twiddling a little switch back and forth.

"H'lo—Hello—H'lo. . . . Ship*ping?* . . . Wll, is thera Rupert Pragman out there? . . . Yess, wll . . . there's a genlmnoutere wansa see'm. . . . What name please? . . . *What name please?*" Charles, who had been sinking into almost dozy restfulness after his search, perceived that the girl had deflected her thin-edged voice toward him.

"Name? . . . Ah . . . Foster . . . ah . . . Foster," he produced, and added, "From the Merchant's Mercantile Association."

The girl turned to the phone again. "Itsa Mister Fawster R. Fawster . . . yais . . . a awri-I . . ." She was looking at Charles again. "He'll be ou'," she promised. They donusually let tha cleyks comouthough, doorinawfisours. . . ."

"Oh?"

There were a few sweetish-tasting moments of waiting, then:

"Mr. Pragman, good-afternoon."

"I—I think you must have the wrong man. I—I—" Pragman produced the words, like a magician so many rabbits, from his throat.

"Oh! No. After our little conversation of this morning, I confess, there might seem little reason for consulting you further. But our policy, sir, is Thoroughness, and we felt we could not act without seeing you again."

"I—I—I—" he was cut off again.

"Quite! Quite!" said Charles Dograr, suddenly assuming an English accent. "If you will step outside to the corridor, where we can talk with perhaps greater freedom, I shall be glad to go further into the matter with you . . . (They were at the door. 'If I go out he'll kill me! If I don't I'll my [sic] job he'll kick up a row and I'll lose my. . . .') . . . certain aspects of the question that are still in need of elucidation."

Glassily moving, Rupert Pragman found they were out in the corridor. Once the door of:

Room 411
Buckeye Belt and Leather Corpn.
F. S. Knox, Prest.

had closed behind them, the disgusting man suddenly seized
Pragman's arm and burst into laughter. It was full five minutes before he could control himself, and then his words came
brokenly between little hiccoughs of merriment, his voice was
weak, his face suffused as of a man who has spent himself with
laughing during an evening of delightful, clean entertainment at

PROCTOR'S FIFTH AVENUE
H i g h - C l a s s   V a u d e v i l l e

(Advt)

He ceased as suddenly as he had begun.

"Where do you live?" he asked.

The abruptness of the question caught Pragman off guard.
Before he could prevent himself, "97 Juniper Street, Yonkers,
New York," he had answered.

"Good!" Charles Dograr had become brisk and business-
like. "You are wondering, no doubt, why I venture to intrude
myself and my affairs upon you during the busiest hours of
your no doubt very fully occupied day. I shall intrude only in
the extent to which these affairs concern you."

He poked an admonitory figure against Pragman's breast
pocket and his eye hypnotically he continued. "Of the extent in

which they do concern you, my dear sir, you are probably not as yet aware. It is my business to inform you.

"As for the 'Merchants' Mercantile Association,' your detective instinct—which, *à propos* (the French words giving a velvety touch to the dialogue) I am delighted, judging from the admirable manner in which you carried off the surprise of our *rencontre* before the telephone girl in the office, to find developed to an unusually (if I may say so) high degree—will tell you that it was but a ruse to justify my presence.

"In fact, sir, my impression of you has been so favorable— vide: one:—(Charles checking off the factors on his fingers as he spoke) your courage and *insouciance* this morning; two:— your quick-wit and *savoir-faire* this afternoon—that it shall be my pleasant duty to report you to the Chief as one most eminently fitted for induction into our organization, and as one thoroughly equipped with the qualifications necessary to the man who will be entrusted with the problem of solving what is perhaps the greatest murder mystery of all time."

Pragman's face gaped before him like the slot of the ornamental letterboxes designed for the Sunset Drive in Sacramento, California. Charles, sensing his ascendancy, paused and drew himself to his full height before he continued.

"I refer, of course—and the secrecy necessary to be observed with regard to this highly confidential statement will mark the implicit trust we place, sir, in you—to the Trulge murder, a case to the solution of which our organization has been called because the police not only of New York but of all the other metropolises—(Charles had not been sure of

the plural form of this word, but he carried it off—he carried it off)—of the world are completely at sea. When can you
begin?"

Words (apologies to Paul Rosenfeld) fluttered like pink
butterflies joyously from Pragman's mouth.

"Are you—are you—" he asked, "from the Searchlight
Detective Agency and Training School?"

Charles' heart leaped proud within him. It had not, after
all, been a wrong guess. He had made it a toss-up between
scenario-writing and detectives.

"Exactly! Exactly!" he replied on a note of enthusiasm. "I
knew I could count on you to understand. At times, in the study
of our thorough-going course in detectiving in all its phases,
your determination may have weakened, the light may have
grown dim before your eyes. But now, now!—now!—you see
the reward!"

And—"The Reward!"—he repeated, producing the badge
which, like the good strategist he was, he had been careful to
procure beforehand.

"You are now,"—pinning the medal to Pragman's vest—
"an operative of the Searchlight Detective Agency, empowered at home and abroad, to retain, suborn, interrogate,
replevin, and proceed to the arrest to, from and of all malefactors, criminals *or* suspected malefactors *or* criminals *or* other
persons known or for good reasons supposed to be enemies of
the Body General, by these presents be it resolved.

"Your salary will be from $3000 to $5000 a year!

"All expenses will be paid!

"You will travel!

"You will see the world!"

He paused. Pragman's heart, like a Strasbourg goose's liver, was feeding on his words.

"Quit your job tonight. Give your employer any excuse you may think of.

"At an hour as yet undetermined, but for the present to be denominated as 'X,' I or another operative empowered to treat with you will visit you at your home at 97 Juniper Street, Yonkers, New York!

"Hold yourself in readiness!

"You will recognize the visitor by the password—'Eggs are indeterminate but fowls are firm.' The operative will reply—'If Moscow reverses, sell at once'!

"Accept no substitute!

"Have you studied the Trulge case?"

Pragman shook his head, chagrined. For a permissible moment, Charles Dograr looked stern. "You must keep *au courant*," he admonished at last, relenting.

He thrust a copy of the *Evening Journal* into Pragman's hands.

"Here! Study this! A detailed report and instructions will be handed you by the operative referred to!

"Meantime. . . Secrecy! . . . Watchfulness! . . . Eternal Vigilance!"

A fleeting handclasp, warm with friendliness, strong with resolution. . . .

A word: "We depend on you!"

And Rupert Pragman rubberly was trying to open the familiar

Room 411
Buckeye Belt and Leather Corpn.
F. S. Knox, Prest.

Charles Dograr had vanished toward the elevators.

7—LIGHT THROUGH FOG

Y ou will observe, then—," the old gentleman halted suddenly, looking down at his young disciple. "Have you
plenty of paper?" he asked.

"Oh! Yes! Yes!" said Charles Dograr, all agog to continue
the fascinating lesson.

"Hm-m-m-m-m. It may seem that we start rather far afield,
but have I proved my fundamental thesis: that Metaphysics, per
se, is intrinsically as precise a science as Physics, since, granting
the division of the senses, each derives, by the same means,
from the Science of Ontology?[1]

"Yes," said Charles Dograr.

"I think I stated too," continued the old gentleman, "the
curious fact—simple enough, but so often overlooked—defin-
ing the difference between these two sciences, namely: that
both, though proceeding by directly parallel methods, make
use of absolutely complementary human equipment—if I may
so state it.

"Roughly, one depends on the mind to the exclusion, if
possible, of the senses—the other on the senses to the exclusion, if possible, of the mind. And *entre parenthèses*, I may say
that the bastard pseudo-science of Psychology falls between
two stools when it tries to straddle the difference."

[1] Springart and Carm, *The Physicist's Handbook*, (Cincinnati, 1914) pp. 137–5; Gorgorza,
La Esencia de las Ciencias, (Valladolid, 1743) vol. 8, ch. xliii.]

"Oh!" said Charles Dograr.

"Now, when two instruments operate by the same method on the same subject, the difference in result, obviously, will be the measure of the difference in accuracy between the two instruments. The difference between the definitions of identical objects or phenomena as stated by each of the two sciences, then becomes an exact indication of the discrepancies in coordination between the mind and senses of man as at present functioning.

"We can," he picked up a half-eaten pork chop and began idly gnawing it as he continued, "go further. Using this difference as a base, we can by a process of mental triangulation[2] similar to that by which the surveyor estimates immensurable distances, conjecture the point at which the two sciences will converge into unity.

"For, obviously, if the two are homogeneous in nature and homogenous in growth, the pinpoint of perfection in both (and consequently in man's function) will be the moment at which each merges into the other.

"Moreover, it is my firm belief that the best way to advance our comprehension of the interrelation between the two sciences is by formulating—just as the economists with their *homo œconomicus*—a conjectural *homo physico-philosophicus*,

---

[2] Federman, *Die Farbrelationem von Raum*, (Leipzig, 1878) p. 57 . . . *"durch die sinnliche Relation des aus der dreidimensionalen Gleiderung gewonnen Koordinationssystems. . . ."* etc. There are interesting foreshadowings of this theory among many earlier students, vide: Lucian, *De Scientia Libidinis*, (Ms. Bib. Nat. Par.) fol. V, pp. xxii-vi, cix-xx, etc.; Hesser, *Zun Alkimie Fundalis*, (Antwerp 1532) who, thinking to develop a system of alchemy, divined instead, almost miraculously, the system of modern thought.

thus predicating, at the very beginning, the perfections that will accrue when the two sciences exact.[3] "I am not the first, I may say," the old gentleman smiled deprecatingly, "to have advanced the possibilities of this method of procedure. But to my knowledge," and his voice rose higher as he spoke, "I am the first who has ever pursued it to any practical end.

"We have established, then, the principal point to be understood in consideration of my invention: That the *homo physico-philosophicus can exist,—that his mind and his senses will act and interact in complete harmony, and that therefor he can be defined as one to whom the Sciences of Physics and of Metaphysics will be synonymous!*"

In his excitement he threw aside the porkchop. "Can exist, did I say?" Leaning forward, he emphasized each word of the sentence that follows by a light tap of the forefinger on the left breast of Charles Dograr. "He *does* exist! I am the *homo phys-ico-philosophicus*–the first perhaps, that has ever existed in the history of man!"[5]

[3]The sense of this passage is obscure. Several variant readings have been proposed. G. C. K. suggests: . . . . "beginning, the exact perfections accrue to the two sciences." Camb. Ed. (L. L. J.) reads. . . . "beginning, the perfect science that this accretion will exact." We give the Ms. reading, though obviously perverted.—Editor.

[4]He refers undoubtedly to Florentia Guillamentius, from whose *Un Leocht Ser Zeltgeis*, (Amsterdam 1688), pp. 971–2, the passage is an almost exact transcription.

[5]Excepting, possibly, Pythagoras. In this connection a 64-page in-12 pamphlet, privately issued in New York, 1907, under the name of René Fonstant and entitled, *"The Kinetic Properties of Form,"* may be mentioned. 'René Fonstant,' it will be remembered, was one of the aliases of the old gentleman. The book is an attempt to modernize the Pythagorean theory of metempsychosis, applying it as a key to the atomic theory.

Charles silently raised a glass of sherry in homage, then drained it. The old gentleman continued.

"Let us now try to understand the hypothetical brain functioning of this man. I have already pointed out the curious fact that in their definition of matter, the Sciences of Physics[6] and Metaphysics[7] differ only in that the first states that some substance as yet undetermined, when combined with *energy*, produces objective phenomena, while the second holds that the same substance, combined with *form*, produces the same result.

"Both, therefor, are negative definitions, and can most advantageously be stated thus:

(Physics):   Phenomena — Energy = Matter   (A)

(Metaphys:)[sic]   Phenomena — Form = Matter   (B)

"Observed phenomena and observed matter are obviously equivalent terms in equation (A) and in equation (B). We can, therefor, subtract equation (B) from (A), and reach the result:

Form — Energy = 0

"Or:

Form   = Energy"[8]

---

[6] Benson and Hedges, *Tobacconist's Guide* (N. Y.).

[7] Thomas More, *De Dementia Mundis* (Oxford, 1577). *Book of Knowledge*, (Int. Book Corp., 1918), pp. 913–27, etc. The book is invaluable, its publishers assert.

[8] As a matter of fact, the invention of various mechanical devices in which the utilization of force engendered was pushed to hitherto unheard-of limits, had already begun

"Really," said Charles Dograr. "I never was very mathematical." He was beginning to feel a bit bored with it all. He glanced tentatively, even longingly, (and was his glance observed?) in the direction of the engine of death, now shrouded under its black cover. The night was like the hair on his scalp and he began to wish once more to be at his post at the oculascope while the old gentleman sent his bulls-eye bullet piercing the walls of distant chambers and the sleepers therein, of whose multiple respirations his fainting senses were now but the echo, slumbrously receding (and had it been only that this fevered desire for action might be born in the young man's brain that the old gentleman had launched on his astonishing burst of rhodomontade?)

And he was still talking. ". . . simple for our *homo physico-philosophicus!* Form equals Energy–naturally. But first let us ask how far we may safely. . . ." (The room whistled with light but through the window Charles saw the loitering night, beguiling, like a Spanish senorita. He felt sleepy. The air was like knives in his nostrils and). The old gentleman was still talking. . . . "whole question of invisibility brings us to—

"Conclusion 3: that *Form is but a kind of inorganic blastomere, of which Energy can be considered as the epiblast*"!

---

to force physicists in general to the consideration of the truth of this or a similar theory. See Signor Storelli, inventor of the Sliding-Arc Water Sphere, in a paper read before the R. I. S. E. M. E., "I personally am convinced that the explanation of the Water-Sphere lies in some kinetic relation, as yet uncharted, between form and energy, per se—the study of which relation and its utilization will be the next great advance in the Science of Physics!"

"Oh! Quite probably! Quite probably!" Charles Dograr agreed, and then began feverishly taking notes.

"Then, if the biological analogy be sound, which I have, to my own satisfaction at any rate, amply proved in practice, it follows that *Form is actually a kind of static growth through which Energy, by a very real form of metastasis, is derived.*

"Energy then, to put it more simply, is merely isomeric Form. And Form, therefor, is capable of indefinite projection through space—*provided that the co-related energy be entirely endogenous!*

"And now—" the old gentleman produced a large diagram (reproduced herewith; see page 79). Then, going to his machine, he opened the stereopticon-like chamber, revealing an intricately interweaving, oppositely-ascending pair of quartz tubes or cylinders, each of which looked rather like the skeleton of a pyramid, ascending in continuous, diminishing, proportionate rectangles "—for the mechanics of the thing. . . ." (And

Charles[9]

[9] began thinking heavily. He had enemies, or rather he was enemies for example the man who had bumped in the gray suit and there had been a guard on the Third Avenue El not to mention the waitress at Childs as some possibility in the conception awakened his brain and he stared assiduously at the old gentleman. One had but to ask apparently in the future he must get the address. 97 Juniper Street? He asked but he said no and.

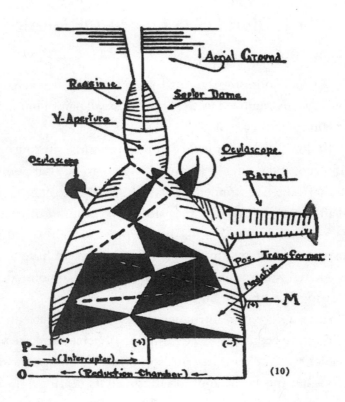

[10] "Look here," he said thickly rising and he waving a sh-h-h hand the old gentleman understanding nodding to the blackdraped engine but with a sly eye: "Take a few hours rest now."

8—"I THINK HE IS LIGHT OF HEART!"

In a small room on the third floor of the house across the way, a lady removed from her eyes a small pair of binoculars, and laid them on a table.

"It don't look as if they'd do much tonight," she murmured half aloud, and yawned. "But Fred is going to be disappointed." Although she had stopped speaking abruptly, closing her ruby lips and firm white teeth almost sternly over the last word, there was a suspended intonation in her voice which would have moved most authors, in describing the scene, to have affixed, immediately after the letter 'd' in the word 'disappointed," the following row of dots: '. . . . .'

Since we are now introducing this lady to the attention of the interested reader, some description of herself and the *milieu* in which we find her is perhaps appropriate—though (if we are to consider the word "appropriate" in all its bearings) the lateness of the hour (it was 4:45 A. M.), the intimacy of the chamber (it was her bedroom) and the negligence of her apparel (she wore only a blue silk chemise and blue satin mules) must deter us from carrying too far our investigations.

In fact, had the reader been led actually to open the door of that chamber at the hour mentioned, the first glance about the walls of the room would have led him (if he be as mature in experience as we suppose he is) to close the door softly and make his way out to the street again (if he be as decent and upright a man as we pray him to be).

Arriving, as we have postulated, in the flesh, the first thing to strike the eye of our reader would perhaps have been the bed. It was large, of imposing structure, covered with a pink silk coverlet. At its head a pink-shaded light cast a seductive glow on the pillows. He would have noticed the washstand, with its soap and basin and towels and oilburning water-heater. He would have observed the pages clipped from *La Vie Parisienne*, *Sans Gêne* and *La Revue Parisienne* that had been tacked along the wall. He would not have failed to remark the photos, in bathing suit, lingerie and the altogether, of the lady herself. His eye, travelling about the room, must surely have encountered the form of its feminine tenant, but by this time the corybantic wantonness of the setting most [sic] have struck some vague but responsive chord in his memory and have driven him from the temple of this modern Cybele, ere her lips had formed the accepted phrase of greeting, "Hello dearie!"

In other words, the lady was a prostitute. In the flesh, the reader must have fled from her—or paid ten dollars to investigate her charms. We see no valid reason why the readers of this book should be otherwise dealt with. On receipt of ten dollars we will forward in plain wrapper a complete and catalogued (illustrated) description of Madame Helène Montmorency.

In the meantime, however, the lady. Drawing one knee— pearl-like, almost translucent in its rounded loveliness—within the circle of her soft white arms, she remained for some time, meditant. Her eyes, dark beneath the flame of her rutile hair; her lips, murmurous with unformed melody; the softened chin;

the tremulous volutes of the creaming throat—all, all revealed her dreams to be of someone dear to her.

Who was that someone—the unknown "Fred" she had previously mentioned?   .

"Put the sheet back over it again all right, anyway,"—she spoke, half at random, to herself. "The kid, too. . . ." Here some unuttered thought made her laugh a moment, gurglingly and low.

Then she was silent again, rocking back and forth in her chair, the white knee still netted in the whiter hands. "But what in the devil can they be up to, anyway? . . . Five o'clock in the morning. . . .

"It certainly beats me!" she concluded, and rose, and yawned. Then, yielding to a sudden impulse, she once more seized the binoculars and directed them at the window of the house across the way.

That impulse was to change the course of many lives, but none to a destiny more bittersweet than her own. For what she saw, as her many-times magnified gaze swept the front of the house, made her start and draw back a moment in alarm—and then, tentatively, as if in response to a signal but half understood and less than half expected, wave an arm in greeting!

Across the dark, deserted slot of Twenty-Third Street, brought close to hers by the magic glass but still veiled by umbriferous night, she saw a face—a young face, but a man's face withal—a face lit with the dignity of desire and beautiful with longing. She saw the face of Charles Dograr, framed in the casement of his chamber window, and the eyes—such eyes as ne'er before had gazed in hers—seemed staring directly at her! It had been an instant. She could not be sure. But then she had seen the handkerchief floating at the tips of his fingers—had seen him wave it at her. She had started back, a prey to a thousand conflicting emotions. Then, as we have seen, tentatively, even timidly she had waved in return. An instant later, grown bolder, her slender hand had drawn a kiss from her imprisoning lips; a breath had wafted it to his. And with dilate eyes she saw the kiss, 'mid a sweet swarm of others, returned to her—seemed, even, to feel them hot upon her cheeks and brow, and lips.

She heard the door of her room open behind her!

"That you, Fred?" she queried, summoning all her woman's will to keep the tremor from her voice.

"Who tha hell did yexpect?" came the coarse reply. And now she turned, riant, assured, drawing down the curtain as she looked at him.

"Well, you never can tell, honey, these days," she replied glitteringly.

"Listen!" said the man savagely. He was blond, large, heavily set. He had thrown himself on the bed. "Listen!" And for a moment she thought he would spring at her. But his manner changed, became secretive. His voice fell to a whisper. *"Been watching?"* he queried.

"Yes."

"Well—?"

"Why, it's just like I said, Fred. There's nothing in it."

"Well, what're they doin' over there, then?"

She faced him, riant, insolent. "You want to know, do you? Well, I'll tell you. They're developing photographs!"

The man spat. "Hell!" he ground out. Then, becoming suddenly suspicious: "Well, whassa big machine for, wit ta cloth over it?"

"That's to print the pictures with, silly." She had affected an air of careless impatience as she spoke, but her eyes watched him furtively. His knowledge was wide, she knew. Had he ever printed photographs? Would he detect her subterfuge?

He seemed to believe, to be convinced. But he took up the strain again. "Well, whadda they woika night for?" he wanted to know. "Listen, Helen, the's somethin going on there, take it from me." She shrugged her shoulders, riant, beautiful, and the man's dull brain told him, and his greedy eyes told her that never before had he found her more maddeningly desirable. "It's the nearest thing to a clue, anyway, that I've struck yet, an the whole Headquarters is woikin ona case. Listen, Helen, if I could put ta hooks inta them two grifters they'd jump me to a Captain right off ta shot. Ta chief is damn' near nuts, what witta papers gassin him an all. Listen Helen. . . ."

He had not, as yet, suspected her. She must lead him on. "I don't give a damn, Fred," she said, drawing near to him, "whether you're a captain or not. It's you I want—you—you!"

Something in her tone must have set him on his guard, for he thrust her from him. "Me, hell!" he grated. An evil light came in his eyes. He seized her wrist, twisted it cruelly. She sank to her knees before him, tortured, but riant still. "Listen!" he ground out. "Look at me, damn you! Are you tryin ta double-cross me? What–were—they—doin–over–there? Come across!!"

The agony of it twisted her supple body like fire but she stared straight at his eyes. They were hard blue like manacles on her tortured soul but she thrust them off.

"Photos—oh! God! Fred! That's killing me! Photographs . . . they were developing . . . photographs . . . photo. . . ."

He thrust her from him with an oath.

"Gimme them glasses!" He rushed to the window. Another oath, as he saw the windows dark. A sigh of relief from her, as she noticed that the face of the young man had been withdrawn. Fred slammed the glasses on the table and turned, like silk on steel, to her.

"Listen girlie," he said. "Get this straight. I'm givin ya tha whole dope. I don't say I know now, but it looks damn funny ta me. These guys sit up all night wrastlin wit ta old Kodak? Mabeso, but every time tey do, why somebody gets moidered somewheres. Now I aint cracked dis yet down to Headquarters. I'm woikin on it alone, see—you an me. If we put it on to dem, it's a stripe for me, see, an a big swell fur coat for you.

"But if you double-cross me," he spat, and stepped closer to her, as she watched him, fascinated. "—if you pitch *me*, girlie—"

His arm flashed out suddenly. There was the smack of a hard fist across a soft cheek, and the lovely form went tumbling to the floor.

He jerked her up. "Don't cry, dearie," he grinned in mock tenderness. "That ain't tha beginning o what I'll do ta ya!"

He held her a moment, staring into her streaming eyes, then shoved her roughly to the bed. She lay limp across the satin coverlet, sobbing.

The man picked up his derby hat and moved to the door. He stood a moment, hand on latch, grinning at her.

"Don't forget now," he grated, in his deadly voice and was gone.

Slowly Helène Montmorency dragged herself to the window, watched Fred stalk up the street. He turned the corner of Ninth Avenue. Dawn was coming. The windows across the way were like fishes' eyes, vacant. Her phantom love had disappeared.

"Oh!" she sobbed. "If he only knew. If only I could tell him! There's danger, and I alone can know of it. I must tell him!" Slowly, as she watched the tears dried and the smiles came back. Tenderly, she tossed a kiss to that silent upper window, and another, and a third.

"I love him," she breathed. "I think he is light of heart!"

The streets grew brighter, she watching. A new day had dawned, for the sleeping city. And a new day, too, a day of love and hope, and joy and fear and hate, was dawning for Helène Montmorency.

And still she stayed there, breathing kisses and passional avowals to her mysterious lover, across the dreary wastes of drab old Twenty-Third Street!

9—INTERLUDE

It was Sunday and the great office buildings honeycombs of silence. People were circulating slowly along the streets of the city except the protuberant man in a brown suit with his deprecative spouse walked along paths tremulous like eggs about to hatch he was rattling his stick against the rusted black railings; the fountain plopped and plashed.

Charles Dograr sat in Madison Square Park like a man in a parachute green-gray-yellow falling reminiscently heavenward his finger between the pages of his book watching the cane an attenuated focus of all the sun in the air spinning the man and his wife and his accordeon [sic] trousers toward where the Garden huzzed treacherously like a longnecked turtle. The circus was there. Adeline.

A slush of silence waded over the Park after the passing of a Fifth Avenue bus. To fling to the moment passing birdly he was fumbling for a dutiful crumb of thought: he had plenty to think about as (glistering like listerine) a page from an old newspaper swished rattling along the path. At an immeasurable distance across Fifth Avenue where (a whirr (the chatter of traffic   GOLDBAUM & BIRNER   enmoiling) of red-   SILKS   yellow axles) winked maliciously into a building-window (through the poignant moment of disparition) as New York again had swooned smotherlingly over him (her face drowning) irremediably (into the freckled

sides of the Flatiron Building). A barb of premonition trans-
fixed his heart. He got up hastily and walked over to the stage
entrance of the Garden.

"I've come to see Miss Adeline Laggick," he announced to
the doorman.

"No visitors allowed."

Charles bowed, crossed the street, disguised himself as a
Western Union messenger boy and presented himself at the
door again.

"Telegram for Miss Adeline Laggick."

"Second tier up, third door from the staircase. It's dressing
room number eighteen."

The long arc of the lower corridors was yellowy dim-
lighted. Here in like crucibles of shadow the animals: he heard
the roof yawn to the growl of a lion, the pad-pad of the tiger's
fringed paws. There was a sweet sickening odor crawling up
everywhere from the straw; a man was mixing bran in a pail;
three or four others among red-painted band-wagons were ras-
tling laughing each other about. The vindictive tail of a panther
flipped along the sketched gray bars of a cage as he passed. Seeing the flat loose sides of the beast its heavy forepaws stretched
past into darkness again on its incessant promenade. His head,
dizzying; like climbing a tree he went up the stairs to the dressing room.

He knocked on the door number 18. A seemingly
impromptu maid opened. He looked in at a bare room, trunks
painted with large white letters, clothes against a wall a mirror
a dressing table electric light. "Telegram," he said. (She was

seated before the mirror in a smudgy kimono pencilling [sic] her lips).

"Oh! Lord! What the devil's up now?" she cried pettishly without turning. "Give me it, Marie." He felt as useless as a gas inspector, standing there in the doorway.

He wanted to see her open the missive. It read (he had stopped along the corridor to scribble it on the telegraph blank he always carried with him):—"Meet me without fail Dyckman Street ferry six o'clock important Cousin Herbert." But she had chucked it unopened into a japanned theatrical makeup box.

She glanced irritably up at him. "Well, what're you waiting for?"

"Any answer?" he replied like a ventriloquist.

"Oh!" She tore open the envelop. An expression of surprise crossed her visage. She reread the screed. "Where did this come from?"

"Twenty-Second Street station."

She was silent a long time, a half smile (or was it, like the carmine flush that mantled her cheeks, the effect of cosmetics only?) on her lips. She roused herself, turning to him, the kimono, unnoticed, falling half open from her exquisite shoulder as she moved. "No. No answer."

She spoke with the decision of a broker, or a woman in love; then, almost as if she owed an apology to the very messenger boy for the curtness of her response—"He—he gave no address," she added hesitatingly. And—"Marie, give this young man a quarter!"

And as the bare yellow door closed him out again into the corridor, he heard her voice, joyously—"Marie, I shall dance this day as I have never danced before!"

And the maid, cajolingly—"Ah! Madame who dance always wiz ze soch gr-rate charm. . . ."

◆

The pain of the long day was o'er. The sky was red, as with blood. Charles Dograr, like a mother in travail, had given birth to six o'clock, and all the timepieces in the city were bawling. She was on the Dyckman Street ferry with him.

◆

They leaned over the rail watching the tasseled foam was hodding on the riverdrift swirled lazily across their bluff bows plunging. The river leaped under the spur of the sun.

◆

"Look!" she cried letting for a moment her small hand touch his arm and softeningly plump it was and ("Shell-like," he thought and really when you saw the flashing longpointed nails faintly corrugated with streaks of light brandished by the taper tenderly-pinchable figures, really because) pinkly translucent he thought as if the palm were lined with mother-of-pearl. He had overlooked what she had said.

It had been something about canoes. Smiling a woman's uncommunicative smile she slowly withdrew her hand. Her manner gave undue importance to the gesture, allowing a her-ringboned section of coatsleeve to stare up again at him star-tledly, [sic] as if it didn't belong there.

"It doesn't matter," he said, like Christ.

"But wouldn't *you*—I don't think you even heard a *word* I said!" she said chidingly smiling.

He smiled shyly and a little fixedly in return and he was to remember the little scurf of powder dustwhite on the edge of her nose.

◆

But as he looked determinedly away from New York—as yet.

◆

The wind had brought her relentlessly against him. One arm was raised to secure her tilting hat. He saw how the move-ment had raised one slimpointed breast in its satin sheath and he thought how easily he could slip his shoulder his hooked arm into the crisphaired forkedopen [sic] hollow of her arm-pit bringing the fullblossomed breasts crushingly against his lips and his loins twisted a little. "Not yet! Not yet!" he almost cried. A woman's body is so always immanent. The ferry chocked into the slip. Bells rang. Gears ground. Chains rattled.

Starters churred in the stopped motors. The sound of feet volleying in the hollow vault of the ferryhouse.

◆

He looked at the sky with a vague recognition, as if he ought to have remembered it, but didn't. The Palisades on their right had shut down on them like a welloiled shutter. She was probably thinking of something. But her climbing legs up the rocky path kept him from her thoughts. He had all the pleasure of going to be happy

Halfway up they paused. It was all green with tree shadows. Officially he put his arm around her and felt her hip lean into his. Through a gap in the branches New York showed her calm riverward face to them, yellow like a sunburnt brow above the blue water. For a moment sensation stopped and he could rest with her; then the sweep of his desire spread again. It was like a gaudy-colored fan between them.

"*Oh*! These *bri*ars," she exclaimed, snatching with an annoyed laugh at her short skirt. They were at the top. With no roof of trees over him, naked-headed under the sky, nevertheless he found himself kneeling beside the silk of her knees to disengage the caught hem. They were so close with their soft curves bubblelike lifting upward into the satin-scented tent of her skirt; he saw the grain of the stocking's weave he was so close: an infinity of minute sparkles like dew following the intertwining shining thread and rounding tighter over the creamy calf. Nothing had ever been sweeter in his eye than that curve and (he could touch it. Yes) feeling his hand cupping to the (slide so easily: up: up to the perfumed salacious taut-tendoned pit back of the knee where: all passions rise and: up where the flesh is firm and warm and (in the river below were prows plunging the soft unresistant water lasciviously creaming back and under from the blunt urging and) his arm hook-elbowed sliding resistlessly up to the groove-muscled thighs (if his lips now?) as "Do you roll your stockings?") he was asking fatuously but he wanted the acquiescence of her voice.

It is not a deed for silence and he looked up at her face bent down over the oh! Pregnable bastions of her breasts.

"*Ev*erybody does, *si*lly!" her voice not as it should was saying. She swept her skirt aside with two hands so that it arced across where (childishly it seemed) bare and tightened waterly over the slope of the thighs.

A dawning maliciousness he read on her face; her eyes were dark with tyrannous expectation. The moment was mal à propos but:

(Without more ado he had clutched and like corseting between his two thumbs the flesh inside her leg yielded up to his lips: he kissed. Something swelled and liberated within him. From now on the little blood-clot would be like a machine: so soft the flesh so indecently soft in its cushioning elasticity that he could bite now to the bone to find some stiffness meeting his: in its cleaving depths he could let his jaws clinch together (and releasing watch the sudden white and the following flowing red that would wave into the bluish hollowed teeth-marks under the film wet from his withdrawing mouth) and:

"*Now* you're being *naugh*ty!" she had said but a gloze of red (as if rending across his eyes) before the unstable whiteness of her skin. He put his arms around her knees and tightened to weaken her columnar uprightness as one might uproot a monument but:

"*No!* You're *hurt*ing me!" with the other arm (but her hand had (caught his arm: he) stared at her face without seeing: it was not yet time but) awkwardly. "I *told* you to *stop!*" she had cried and, "I wouldn't have *come* her with you if I'd thought you were going to act like *that!*"

But:

◆

And:

◆

Then:

◆

Afterwards and all that had flowed away and they were sitting on some coarse crisp yellow grass on the edge of the rock. The valley came up at their eyes like a rush of air. There was an as it seemed specially provided dusk and a slow-motion Albany steamer amid a diagram of ripples was headed interminably upstream. It *is* browlike. As when (slowly) in darkness

one comes to perceive the objects about him (but this darkness
that we know redshot and dancingly as the woman Time jogs
on her elbow) he discovered himself lying on his back with
(she was lying beside him smiling) New York shiningly like a
brushstroke long yellow across the lower sky.

◆

She was satisfied but he felt her to be an intrusion but her
legs crooked about his consciousness.

◆

He thought of the Old Gentleman. Murder, like the villain in the piece, he dragged a little theatrically across his
mind. It was only to give a semblance of importance to his
complete comfortableness. Besides, somewhere in that shuttling strip of (picked out with purple) yellow an unknow [sic]
man 3 millimetres tall sat in his window looking out at the
Palisades and:

◆

"What shall I *call* you you are not Cousin Herbert of *course*
you know I know *that*?"

◆

"Your eyes are like Lake Geneva deep at their bottom is a floor of ice in their cooling blueness my red thoughts are refreshed I would wound you."

◆

"Your eyes are like the daisies of the field you see thousandly and your breasts on their red-blue hubs are as two white chariot wheels that roll me beneath your body."

◆

"Your breasts are like the prows of two pink ships that plunge creaming into my heart's center."

◆

"It's *beau*tiful here isn't it *I'll* tell what we'll come here some *night* and I'll do my *dance* for you!"

◆

"Your shoulders cape about me like the flower of Isis their fragrance shuts out light and darkness through the coiled channels of your navel I shall blow kisses to your heart."

◆

"Your navel is the pin-pricked center whence your beauty is the radius of my world your hips I see faint with many colors are the ovate cup of my desire."

◆

"Your hips are as a vase my glory my pride my courage shall find root and flourish there."

◆

"I think men are so *silly* they always want to *argue* about something even when it's about me I find it *tire*some but I love you but I could *hurt* you."

◆

But and both talking neither hearing the other a man had appeared behind them a man black against the sky and from his pose the tapping stick one saw he was blind and deaf and voiceless. Neither saw him. He stood outlined black against the sky. "Death is a complete quiescence," thought McDowell and, "Man, no more than a tree, a stone, shall ever suffer death, save in part, and glancingly. After vomiting, for instance. Not unwisely, in an earlier day, did they speak of men vomiting forth their souls. And the more intimate ejaculations as well. So the seed of life is death and of death, life. X within O—that is the symbol of the universe." And:

◆

"Your hips are like the soil of Heaven your legs like the branching of two white rivers enclose the island of my paradise."

◆

(Sometimes (I think it was I who sat there on the Palisades and lying beside me that wide-cheeked soft-lipped deep-eyed loose-bodied slut waiting smiling for my (or for his) caresses and) sometimes) Charles Dograr: thrillingly and afar he had for a moment heard the march of Life about him (or was it the tapping stick McDowell?) and with a sense of infinite foreboding he had (as you (or I) sitting here in our orchestra chairs (suppose you or I) were to rise and step forward to the scene taking the place of the hero?) Charles in a mood of deep profundity: "I shall not live long," he had said: "in no one of my dreams can I see myself old I shall not live long not more than 250 pages": he had said and (suddenly (dazzledly) [sic] as one rising from (is it the Seine this long blue laughing?) from the water's depth into shattering sunlight he (thrusting up through the perfume of some unknown woman's hair her body sweeter far than he) found himself) sitting there and:

◆

Imperceptibly the Night brooding from the trees (the Night) kneading the white woman's body graying into the gray receiving earth and:

◆

"Death encases Life," and McDowell and: "Man loves not so much with the desire to be a father as to be a grandfather. We progress in alternate interlacing loops, the body the adumbration of the sequitive [sic] sperm. Life is an entail on the estate of Death," and:

◆

The blue the (drifting he knew it was Sunday and) "Adeline! Adeline!" he cried frenziedly. She raised her head to stare at him. "This is the last time! My youth is passing. This is the last time! The last time!" and:

◆

McDowell had stepped unperceived (and touching his tapping stick her breasts her body her belly) and:

◆

"*I was* not *made* for fina*l*ity I'll wear my *white* dress when we come *again*, and:

◆

"The last time! This is the last time! and (bloating before (his eyes rent apart) the white the (he stared a moment down to the twisting membranous structure) and then: "This is the last time!") it was (he saw distinctly) a fountain blue-white shot from the wound: rose quivering. It sprayed out across the sky. The drops fell: becoming petals; becoming plunging flames: canopied down on her. He was (sprawling on four legs like an animal) regarding nothing.

McDowell had gone on. His stick tap-tapping receded among the cliffs. Charles Dograr saw nothing. There was a flash of satiny white among the trees.

"Adeline! Adeline!" he called into blankness. He rose and fled.

She heard his footsteps tumbling away among the rocks. A dark stranger came and stood by her side.

10—EIGHTEEN MEN

It was in Stockholm that I met Fernand Leger, and under rather amusing circumstances. I was strolling one morning on the *Bradgvur*, that most charming of all promenades, when a small man, with narrow head and lank black hair, approached me. I saw at once that it was Leger, and assumed that he, though we had never met, had also recognized me.

" 'He accosted me, and with any prelude, demanded, "Are you a philistine?"

" 'It will perhaps be understood that I did not 'catch on' at once. He was evidently quite terribly in earnest–so much at least was clear.

" ' "Why—why—" I stuttered, when he cut in abruptly: "Well come up to my studio and take a look at my cat. I'm afraid it will die!"

" 'Naturally I went—not to see the cat, but to see his pictures, and was amply rewarded. As it turned out, of course, the explanation was simple, as all explanations are. In his excitement, coupled with his lack of facility in the Swedish tongue, he had confused the word for philistine—'*Sturvagsdt*,' with '*stavgardt*,' meaning veterinary!

" 'Nevertheless,—as Leger himself admitted when I laughingly taxed him with it—the incident has to me always seemed a strikingly just epitome of his artistic principles. . . .' "

There was a long vague pause for fumbling among the leaves. "M-m-m-m., . . . ah!" and—

" '. . . was his terse and nervous prose, and his astonishing gift of mother-wit, rather than any social graces, that procured Max Beerbohm his invitation to the *soirée* at the d'Alençons, for he had an unpleasant tendency toward kleptomania that made his friends a little uneasy in his. . . .' "

"Here!" said Charles. "Let me read it myself."

Asa Huddleberry, filled with a bulbous delight, handed over the manuscript. He was a critic on the Forum, or was it the Dial?

"What do you think of the title?" he demanded. " 'From A Critic's Diary'—eh?"

Charles looked up to find the man's large, flaccidly intense eyes swelling at him. He laid the bulky sheaf on the floor. "Oh. . . ." he said.

I have remarked that sometimes I think it was I who sat one rose-scented evening on the Palisades beside the girl Adeline and indeed in many ways this Charles Dograr was very like myself.

He was awkwardly conscious of people. He felt ticklishly their glances. He was lumberingly docile at times and at times fanatically precise.

His morals, his ethics, his philosophy had not as yet sharply emerged for his mind was still clouded by strange, volumi-nously sweeping ideas of which his most tenaciously revered was a belief that the operation of the world's forces on him would combine in his own preservation and advancement. He had abiding faith in his own ability and in what we (but he never) would call his luck. And he forced himself almost consciously to strengthen that faith, with a vague sense that if he could make it strong enough not even Fate would have the heart to disabuse him of it.

This childish tendency to animate the inanimate—to motivate the immutable—to render scrutative the inscrutable–was everywhere characteristic of him. If people seemed poignantly alive to him, objects and even objectives were more than alive. Four thousand years ago he would have been a priest of Isis; and now not a packing-box, not a cobblestone of the roadway, still less the Force that made his ambiance, but was endowed, in his philosophy, with Mind and Will.

The effort of his logic was to discover, not the reason, but the reasoning of Things.

Nevertheless, the murder of Edward Trulge, coupled with the two or three that swiftly followed (into collusion in which he had been so cleverly tricked by the old gentleman) had disturbed him greatly. But now he was sitting in Asa Huddleberry's studio in the rooming house, listening with marcescent interest to the other's volubility.

"I should like," Huddleberry was saying, "I should like to write a detective story—a mystery story. . . . But one in which no one should know what crime had been committed—nor who had committed it. . . ."

"That's true of all crimes, isn't it, rather?" asked Charles and watched himself inject a careless laugh, like a hypodermic, into the man's mind. But:

"No one. . . . There should be a dream quality about it all. . . ." His eye lighted; a rising enthusiasm informed his customarily level tones and he waved his long thin hands in wider gestures—"A dream quality, yes; a brooding sense of Something—no one quite knowing what–but Something dread, and menacing, and terrible. A Something that sets all the boasted power of civilization at naught—," he raised his hand as Charles gave evidence of being about to speak, "—at naught, and mocks the puny strength of men. . . ."

"After all," murmured Charles comfortingly to himself, "how puny the little things really are. I *do* get foolish about them." He looked with renewed lightheartedness at Huddleberry, lying there on the crimson chaise longue, the thin figure of him wrapped in his purple dressing gown, and almost took out his pencil and note book like a reporter, as the man went on.

"It shall be my greatest work, that. I see them now in my mind's eye, my characters as I shall write them—small, busy important silhouettes against the black shadow of Fate. . . . They move about, fussily occupied with their lilliputian affairs—beautiful fragile women . . . men evanescently powerful in the affairs of nations themselves soon—ah! soon to crumble into the forgetting dust. . . . Men, women. . . ."

"Don't you think," cut in Charles, forgetting he was interrupting, for a new idea had struck him, "we often confuse permanency with importance in a curiously illogical way? Isn't it often the very impermanence of the thing which makes its importance?

"Man lives his slender span and dies—and it is just that his span is short which gives his death real importance. That's why fresh strawberries are important. A hundred years' erosion crumbles a tower, and so does a thunderbolt—in half a second—and therein lies the importance of the thunderbolt. How unimportant man would be, if he lived a thousand years!

"But still. . . . A telegraph pole, for instance. . . . No. . . . And yet . . ." He relapsed a moment, and the Great Critic, seizing the occasion, went on:

"Men, women, statesmen, courtesans, plotters. . . . and yet, in the mind of each the dread questions are constantly impending—'What is it that threatens?'—'Who the murderer?'—'Where the scene of the tragedy?'—'Shall it be I who will strike the fatal blow?'—'Or shall I receive it?' . . ."

He paused again, staring dramatically at the corner of the ceiling. "And the end—dramatic, inevitable, but veiled in mystery. . . . 'Was there a murder?'—'Who was the victim?'—they shall ask, my characters. And as each sinks shudderingly to sleep—'Was it I who killed, last night as I thought I slept?'—'Am I, even now, am I dead?' . . . Ah! Yes! It shall be my greatest work, that. It would go well in the American Mercury, don't you think?[1]

Charles, who had been chewing his underlip this while in a meditative frenzy, now sprang suddenly to speech. "No. . . ." he cried. "Don't you see? As I said, a telegraph pole is permanent. If anything *could* make a man important, it is his

[1]Var. 1915 ed. ". . . . in the *Smart Set*, don't you think?"]

impermanence. And it does, among his fellows. You carry a basket of eggs more carefully—but not because they are more important—than a basket of potatoes. The eggs, however, seeing themselves cushioned with straw and handled gently, are likely to get pretty pompous about it. So with ourselves. Man's great fragility, and the consequent delicacy necessary in handling a human being lest one inadvertently destroy him, lead us—though quote fallaciously—to consider him very important indeed. But it is when man tries to struggle with true permanence that he becomes ridiculous. Even in small things—as dozens of people have pointed out. For instance: every locomotive that is built means that all men die a little. Do you see what I mean?"

He looked up hopefully. The afternoon trembled. Huddlebery [sic] was frowning.

"What," he asked, "has all this about locomotives got to do with my story?"

"Oh!" Charles re-collected himself, as after a leap. "The story. . . . Murder, wasn't it? I think there are only two people who could write a murder story—the murderer and the victim. For example," he had risen and was at the door, "suppose I were to commit a murder tonight, I would probably then be able to write a good story—from the standpoint of the murdered. If I murdered you, then you would be in the best possible position to write from the standpoint of the murderer."

"Oh! Well," Huddleberry commented petulantly. "If you will try to be clever. . . ."

"Not at all!" Charles himself had been frightened by the

sudden firmness of voice as he had pronounced the words. Huddleberry, however, had not observed. He went away relieved, dragging the bloody word behind him.

That night, however, after the switch had been closed for the eighth time, and Charles still was fiddling with the adjustor-screws, the old gentleman remonstrated mildly.

"Not that I mind," he explained, "only the continued drain on the current might cause comment. That light-box uses a powerful lot of juice. What is it, my boy?"

"Do you know the address of the New Republic?" asked Charles. "I've already been through the Liberator, Nation, Aesthete, Dial and Vanity Fair. The man I'm looking for I don't know where he hangs out."

The old gentleman cast a sly grin downward.

"Your literary friend?"

"There are seven incentives to murder," Charles replied. "So far I've tried three: curiosity, sex-fatigue, and boredom." He patted the focal barrel with comforted eyes. "What's up tonight?" he asked.

The old gentleman opened a brief-case containing maps, diagrams, key-molds, etc. "Well," he began. "I think we'd better rehearse the City Mercantile Bank affair. . . ."

"How many?"

"Eighteen men. The night watchman, four special police, the driver and two guards of the armored car, the teller and assistant teller of the bank, the agent of the Burgeson, Rich Company, our two grifters and the driver of the car I've engaged. . . ." The old gentleman paused, smiling softly up at Charles. "It's always better to get rid of one's accomplices, don't you think?"

Charles nodded grimly. "That makes only fourteen," he commented.

The old gentleman waved a hand. "Well, and the usual number of innocent bystanders," he explained. Charles nodded comprehension.

"Eighteen. . . ." he murmured.

They were silent a moment. A moment, compassion sat heavy on the withers of Charles Dograr's pride. His jaws flattened with pity. The old gentleman observed, and his gaze fell, like a caress from his crooked old fingers, on the wavy locks of our hero's careless head and internally he gave unctuous approval. Then Charles was brusk again.

"I noticed the car downstairs."

"The Hispano–yes."

"Fast work then—eh?"

"It may be. I thought we'd better be sure. It means nineteen millions."

Charles leaned back in his chair. "In gold?"

"Gold coin."

"What time?"

"The armored car with the shipment comes to the bank at exactly midnight."

"Tomorrow?"

"Yes."

There was silence. The heavy yellow brilliance of the room showered like whispering gold on the two. "Nineteen millions. . . ."

"That's enough for a while, eh?" urged the old gentleman. His eye grew suddenly waterily piteously beseeching.

"We might go away for a time. . . . eh, Charles? With nineteen millions. We'll buy a yacht, what do you say, Charles? I saw the very thing in the harbor yesterday, coming in from Long Island. . . . Gibraltar . . . the Mediterranean. . . . Monaco. . . . Suez. How would you like that, Charles? With your old partner. . . . Alone. . . . Ah! . . ." He had flopped forward on the floor.

On his knees on the floor before Charles amazed, and clutching for his hand like an old woman in a Victorian novel. "Just we two, Charles. Alone there . . . on the blue water. I have dreamed of it! I have longed for it—haven't you seen?—since that first night when we—murdered that man out in Union Hill—we, together.

"Must I confess? He was the first . . . the first time I had ever raised my hand to kill! It was your young fiery energy that nerved me to it!" He gave way to a fit of throaty laughter. Charles felt his thighs prickle into gooseflesh. "But that night—that night, I could have dipped my hands into his warm blood—dipped it up with my two hands and blessed you with it, to consecrate our love. Charles, do you hear? Our love!"

His eyes glared wildly. Charles, drawn back deep in his chair, saw them as a man, alone on a narrow road at night, sees the headlights of a motorcar approaching swiftly, roaring.

And the old gentleman's voice went on, the words coming hoarsely as if some hot inner blast were forcing them through the taut channels of his throat. "You know—you must know that I love you! My money! The ardor of my soul! The pride of my intellect! I throw them all at your feet! Charles! . . . (There was an air of theatricality about it all. Mae West in a more advanced moment might have done the scene. Charles waited). . . . Charles! Ah! Charles! We shall defy them all! We will shrivel their brains! Like burnt walnuts! And blood! Blood! Blood!"

He was scrambling to his feet now, his hand crawling toward the boy's planed face.

But Charles now (the moment of horror passed) could almost have laughed, in fact did—insofar as a twisted contortion of the lips, a flaring release of the tensed facial muscles can be called laughter.

He saw with a cold skilled eye the sweat that stood on the old gentleman's forehead, saw the sagging, chattering, lecherous mouth.

And still—"Nineteen millions! It shall be yours and nineteen more, and ninety more as well . . . and all the wealth of Ind. . . . All the jewels of Araby! All, all yours . . . if you but say one word—one word! Ah! Charles! Speak! Speak! . . ."

Charles for a moment sat on the top of the world as (with a decided gesture) like a man putting out a candle he extinguished all emotion, pushing the old gentleman pivotting away.

"What nonsense!" he rasped. And, with the naked assurance of youth, "How about this City Mercantile Bank? Let's stick to business."

The moment that followed must be allowed to weigh with centuries. Man is the toy of Fate, but the emotion within him is like the gravity wheel that, once whirling, propels the child's locomotive up impossible slopes. Arrested, in the one case it crumples the painted plaything—in the other it disrupts the mind and all the plans of men. During that moment the old gentleman had turned his head away, moving his hands across his features like a quick-change artist preparing for the next act.

Then his head rotated on his wrinkled neck. He was seen to be smiling.

"Ah! yes!"—but his voice came gaspingly—"The eighteen men!" (But, "Nineteen!" a demoniac whispering in his brain.)

"That's better!" approved Charles, uncomprehending.

"We'll rehearse tonight."

"How about the three grifters? They all here?"

"In the next room—" Each word had been like clicking a camera shutter. Now his voice broke. And—"Ah! Charles!" once again he was pleading. "The world shall ring with our names, if you but speak. . . . Dograr—sweet sound!—and Picrolas; indivisibly joined to the fat world's horror. . . . Dograr and Picrolas! . . . Picro. . . ."

"Picrolas!" The boy's voice blanched. "Picrolas!!" And the air in the silent room rang like the lip of a bell at the fated syllables and fear ran down through the boy's belly like a skewer through butter. "Picrolas! You–are—Picrolas?"

The old gentleman's face before him was like a knot of green and yellow yarn, untwisting. But the mouth preserved its deadly, even smile.

"You know. . . . You have heard . . . of Picrolas?"

The voice came to him distantly; the smile poniarded his

vision. Who—who living had not heard and, hearing, feared the dread name? Who, as the arch-fiend's tale of crime and desolation had unrolled before the eyes of a startled world, had not felt his eyes grow hot with tears—his heart cold with shame that humanity could harbor so deadly a viper. Men, hearing his iniquities, had sworn that no mother surely, but some devil must have borne him. Frail women's hair had grown white in a single night, simply at reading a newspaper account (and one no doubt censored) of but one of his misdeeds.

Picrolas! Charles felt his courage shrivel now. He shuddered, and the man's grinning face loomed evilly before him.

Two months they had been together now and their crimes had been many and foul enough, as they wielded the x-ray bullet.

But it had been (or Charles had thought it so) lighthearted and young. He had quieted his soul—the old, old story!—with a list of his misfortunes, with a tale of the world's misdeeds. He pictured himself a latter-day cavalier, a modern Robin Hood, astride the machine as the others bestrode their horses. He had told himself that he had robbed the rich to feed the poor. He had—ah! now, with a sickened courage he looked back at it all; he knew now the hideous brain that had urged him on; he saw himself for the fool that he had been.

"Picrolas!"

The old gentleman's smile took on a metallic brilliance. "You—fear—Picrolas?" he asked softly.

The boy was beyond words.

"Say but one word. . . ." the voice came softly, cajolingly,

"One word, and you need not fear him." Under it all was the grimace.

"No! No! Come what will I—" Charles Dograr had risen to his feet. The old gentleman's hand halted him.

"Sh-h-h-h!"

Someone was knocking gently at the door. A moment, when both stared at the other. Then Charles Dograr rose, strode across the room. Anything was better than this inactivity! He opened. Three faces emerged in the gloom—the faces of men steeped in vice, hardened in crime.

They were the three accomplices of the multiple murder the old gentleman had planned for the morrow night.

At another time, Charles would have smiled with mocking courage at their twisted lips, glittering eyes and cut-throat visages—would have vaunted himself for the power he held over them and their ilk.

Now, he could hardly keep countenance before them, for the shame that clamored at his heart. One spoke:

"Whinever yeze arre ready sorr, thin we do be surely," he announced in his laughable Irish brogue. It was a burly, broken-nosed ruffian.

Another, dark, thin, venomous, concurred. "Sure, Let's get-a da woik done. It be much-a late-a." One saw he was of Italian origin.

"Come in, gentlemen." The old gentleman welcomed them with ironic courtesy, but his eye bored ever at Charles. "Sit down."

And then (perhaps God, looking down, may have (no

other, in the sleeping city, could have) seen in that lit room) three brutish men and a brown-haired, fair-faced boy, coached and guided by a wry-eyed old gentleman, went through the preparations for a great crime.

It might have been a game they played, for all evidence to the casual eye (if the casual eye could have overlooked the grim, set faces of the participants, and the anxious instructions of the old gentleman).

First, maps appeared. All the possibilities of the locality were canvassed—even, with chairs and desk and cushions, a miniature map of the scene was made. Then, down to the smallest detail, the part that each man was to play was memorized, the old gentleman supervising. And strange it was to see these blackguards, as each his turn devolved, rise like schoolchildren to recite his lesson. There was much they did not understand.

"Sure, I get-a you. I drives around-a tha corner and-a—"

"No! Not around it. Drive to the corner and stop there!" corrected the old gentleman. "In that way you block both approaches."

"All-a right-a," the Italian assented, it seemed to Charles with an ill grace. "I drive to tha corner-a. An' I jumps out wit me gun."

"Only don't worry about your gun," advised the old gentleman impatiently. The ruffian stared.

"You said-a dey was eighteen o' dem!"

"That'll all be taken care of." Proudly, Picrolas patted the barrel of the x-ray gun. "I will take care of that."

"You? But yez said, sorr, that yez wouldn't be there surely."

"I won't." The men looked bewilderedly at each other. Charles smiled. The old gentleman turned to him and for a moment their glances met in the old derisive camaraderie.

Then Charles hardened and he turned away. But, for a long time, the old gentleman's eye, unnoticed, was pinned to the young man's face.

Charles had been thinking he noticed something that recollected the face of one of the men to his mind. The man wore a derby hat.

"Haven't I seen you somewhere?" he asked. It was a burly, swaggering fellow.

"Me?" The man pictured surprise. "Naw. I just got in from Niagara Falls today."

"Oh?" Charles thought little more of it. And yet, in the back of his brain as, glibly, he ran through the recital of his part of the crime's consummation, there lingered a faint, evasive memory. A blonde man . . . with a derby hat . . . he had walked in fear . . . of what? . . . one early morning. . . .

"You were never in New York before?"

The fellow shook his head negatively.

Half an hour later, the old gentleman professed himself satisfied with the rehearsal and dismissed them.

"Till tomorrow!" Then he turned to Charles. "Do not go, Charles. One word before . . ."

Bruskly, Charles tore his sleeve from the man's grasp; he spoke not a word in reply, but signalled ahead to the man in the derby hat.

"Wait a minute there," he called. "I'll walk down with you."

Left alone, the old gentleman walked heavily across the room until he stumbled almost blindly against the mechanism of the x-ray rifle. He laid his head between his arms on the polished surface. For a time, he wept. Then, suddenly, he raised his head again and his face was horrible to behold. And he raised his clenched hands to Heaven, and his voice came choked with passion.

"Fool!" he gasped. "Twice-triple accursed fool! You spurn me–me, Picrolas! Ha! Ha! You fool, know you not that the power still rests here—with me? Nineteen shall die tomorrow! Nineteen! Here—I swear it! Yourself—you have sealed your doom! Tomorrow's sun shall be your last, or Picrolas is forsworn!"

11–YONKERS—AND WEST

(*a*) Mr. Rupert Pragman put the bottle of milk under his left arm and opened the door with his right. Hurriedly he entered the house. His wife was standing impatiently in the diningroom.—"Hurry up and sit down to your dinner. The nice tunafish on toast I made that you like'll be all cold," she said.—"Did anybody come while I was away?" asked Mr. Pragman.—"No. I think that detective stuff of yours is all a fake," she said. "Sit down to the table," she added.—"Well, all right," Mr. Pragman agreed. They sat down and ate the tunafish on toast.—"It certainly was pretty good," said Mr. Pragman afterward.

(*b*) "Well, let's see what we can get on the radio," suggested Mr. Pragman to his wife.—"All right, Rupert," said she. Just then there was a knock on the door.—"You go see who it is," said Mr. Pragman.—"No. It's your turn," said his wife. He opened the door. A stranger stood on the doorstep. Summoning up all his courage, Mr. Pragman proposed, "EGGS ARE INDETERMINATE BUT FOWLS ARE FIRM." The stranger bowed. He was a distinguished-looking foreigner.[1] He spoke with a slight accent.[2] "IF MOSCOW REVERSES SELL

---

[1] This, the astute reader need hardly be reminded, was undoubtedly a disguise.

[2] The assumption of a foreign accent is a familiar device among detectives, having for object the deception of their prey. In this they attain at times to a high degree of proficiency.

AT ONCE!"—"Come in," said Mr. Pragman.—"We have no time to lose," said the stranger.—"Just a minute till I get my hat," said Mr. Pragman. He got his hat. They went out together. Mrs. Pragman, when left alone, sat down by the radio. She began fiddling with the dials. Two minutes later the machine shuddered and burst into flames. At the same time a heavy brilliance scalloped her brains. The poor woman was dead.[3]

(c) Pragman and the stranger got onto the Subway.—"I suppose you're from Foster R. Foster," asked Pragman timidly.—"Ssh! That is not his real name," said the stranger. "His real name is Charles Dograr!"[4]—"He told me he was working on the Trulge Murder Case," said Pragman.—"He was," said the stranger.[5]

(d) "Come in here," said the stranger, pausing before a pawnshop when they had got to Chicago. They went in and

[3]Was this caused by some as yet uncomprehended combustive capacity inherent in the construction of the radio? Or was it a magnetic diffraction of the rays of the x-ray bullet as the old gentleman, even then, searched for the brain of Charles Dograr? The details, though scanty, of the good lady's death would perhaps render the latter hypothesis more probable.

[4]This is astonishing! Obviously, someone has been working on the Trulge case without the concurrence, perhaps even without the knowledge, of the author. The complete ignorance on the part of Mr. Coates of the most elementary principles of plot construction, apparent through the book, is here devastatingly revealed. The reader, left to his own devices in identifying the stranger, will perhaps do well to assume that it is none other than the missing Herbert Trask. Thus the introduction of a new character is avoided at so late a moment.

[5]—"Well, I thought as much," said Pragman.—"We have got to go to Chicago," said the stranger. They got off at the Grand Central and bought two tickets to Chicago. As there happened to be a train leaving they got on and went to Chicago.

the stranger bought a little gilt locket. They went out in the
street again and opened it. In the back was a picture of a little,
fair-haired girl. The stranger looked at it for some time. "We
must hurry," said he at last. They turned down a side street.

(e) Toward the end of Halstead Street, somebody shot
at them from an upper window. The stranger preserved his
sang-froid.—"Take the number of that house," he said. Pragman took the number down in a little notebook he always carried. The stranger paused at an ashcan. He pulled out a worn
old broom. With a magnifying glass he studied the handle.
Then he went to a drugstore and bought some bichloride tab-
lets.—"These are a deadly poison," he said, showing them to
Pragman and smiling mysteriously.—"Oh! Are they?" asked
Pragman.—"Let us go in and buy a couple dozen bananas,"
said the stranger. "We have a long journey before us." They
went in and bought the bananas. Coming out of the store, a
dark-bearded man ran past them and disappeared in an apartment house, crying: "Eighteen men! Eighteen men!" It was
only one of the curious events of the day.

(f) Dawn found them in Erie, Pennsylvania. The stranger
told Pragman to wait a minute while he went into a grocery
store. Pragman waited and the stranger went into the grocery
store. He conversed for a long time with the proprietor. When
he came out he had a can of tomatoes and looked pleased.—"I
had to buy these tomatoes so as he wouldn't get suspicious," he
explained. "But I found out the man we are after is an old fellow, very mathematical, and he deserted his wife six years ago in
this town. What will we do with this can of tomatoes?"—"Eat

them?" asked Pragman.—"What we better do, we better go see this man's wife. She lives right around the corner," said the stranger. "Have you got the number of that house in Chicago? he added.—"No 436," replied Pragman.—"It's the same number. Wait here till I get the morning editions," said the stranger. They were full of all the details about the Nine Prominent Critics Die By X-Ray Bullet, and it went on to relate how reason shuddered when the city waked up today to find that such men as Harry Hansen, William Soskin, Heywood Broun, Bruce Gould, Waldo Frank, Henry Seidl Canby, Asa Huddleberry and James Thurber and George Jean Nathan were made the victims of a dastardly attack late last night and the police were hopelessly at sea because no motive could be imagined for the murders unless by the Communists from Moscow. The stranger looked worried. Then his brow cleared.— "Well, anyway, Adeline is safe," he muttered.[6]— "Do we go see the wife?" queried Pragman.— "No. We have to hurry back to New York. I have got to report to the Chief," said the stranger. "You come along too."

(g) When they got to the station they found the next train was an hour late. They sat in the waiting room to wait for it. "What do you say we eat that can of tomatoes?" asked Pragman.—"Oh! What the hell do I want with the damned tomatoes?" asked the other.—"Well, I will eat them if you don't want them," said Pragman—"No, you won't either," said the stranger. So saying, he drew his arm back and flung the can

[6]This dissipates all uncertainty as to the identity of the stranger. It is indubitably Herbert Trask. He, too, is probably in love with Adeline.

of tomatoes away from him. Unfortunately, or fortunately as events later turned out, the can smashed through a window in the waiting room and landed in the face of a man who, unknown to them, had been regarding them all along. There was a great uproar at this. Pragman and the stranger rushed outside to see what was the matter.

(*h*) When they got outside, the Station Master was helping the man who had been hit to his feet. When he saw them he rushed up to them.—"Get out of here," he cried angrily. "You pretty near broke the face off of our Superintendent of Schools."—"No, we won't get out. We have got our tickets," asserted Pragman. The Station Master was about to commence an angry retort, when the stranger, who had been closely regarding the supposed Superintendent of Schools, rushed over to his side.—"So he calls himself the Superintendent of Schools, does he?" he asked sarcastically. "Well, us detectives know him as Denver Mike!" And without more ado he pulled off the false beard off the trembling culprit's face and revealed him in his true colors.

(*i*) When the man had been put into the patrol wagon and driven off, the stranger turned to Pragman.—"This changes everything," he confided. "This guy Mike is mixed up in the Trulge case too and I have been looking for him a long time and now that I found him I better stay here and give him the Third Degree. Now you go on to New York and deliver this report to the Chief." So saying, he handed Pragman the report.—"What will I do after that?" asked Pragman.—"Well, you better go home and wait there," said the stranger.—"All right," agreed Pragman. But just as he was going to get on the train, the stranger came running after him.—"Wait a minute," he said. "Go to this address and take a room there and watch what happens. Use the name of Edward Sykes. I will come back there tomorrow." So Pragman got on the train. When he had found a seat, for the train was moderately crowded, he looked at the piece of paper where the address was written. It was on West Twenty-Third Street and more mysterious still if the number of the house could be revealed it would be found to be the same place where Charles Dograr and the old gentleman were now living!

12—TANGLED TRAILS

When the Bat breaks prison
Bill Lawson begins a long
chase with a strange ally.
Peter Gerringer sees a man skulking around an empty house. Inside
he finds another man and volunteers to help if there is danger. The
man leaves him in a locked room and fails to return. Gerringer finds
a murdered Chinaman in the next room and his own hat and stick
smeared with blood. Another Chinaman appears and proves to be
the brother of the dead Chinaman. Gerringer and the Chinaman
chase the murderer in Gerringer's car. Bill Lawson is found in an
alley in a semi-comatose condition. The mark of a spider has been
burned on his forehead. All three give chase. Gerringer is pursued by
another car. Gerringer shot and car ditched, one Chinaman killed.
While dying tells Gerringer murderer is a man named Clay. Sir
Reginald McCloskey's country place in Barsetshire is broken open
and robbed. Peter Graham on liner bound for Shanghai becomes
acquainted with Moore and daughter Wanda. Also German named
Schœnberg. Moore is invalid with weak heart. Moore quarrels with
Schœnberg and dies. Matty Josephson is seen at Monte Carol, clad
in rags but playing for huge stakes at chemin de fer. News arrives
that the mysterious Isma is at the head of a great Bolshevist plot in
Philadelphia, Pa. Wakes at night and finds man in room.

Graham stepped forward.

"What are you doing here?" he demanded, a grim menace
in his lowered voice.

Up over the edge of the box slid a tiny, inquisitive head. It
was followed by the sinuous body of a little yellow snake.

The Hindu hesitated an instant, read death in Graham's blazing eye, and nodded slowly.

"Kill it then—"

"Honorable sir—"

"Kill it, d—n you!" Graham blazed at him. He jabbed the revolver forward.

As he passed, Graham touched him on the arm. "And tell the man who sent you," he added, "that I am going to get him for this—and for other things."

A few hours later Gerringer glanced at his watch and rose to his feet. Nowhere in the shifting, glittering throng had he been able to catch a glimpse of Wanda Moore. Graham threw down the paper and addressed himself to the dishes his water was setting before him, ruminating over the business as he ate.

Like most men gifted with the finer kind of (But the Giverny air is the spawn of silence as: the night dripping dropping on her senses (the mill for example) and like the moonlit ripple curling in the wake of the schooner Night, drifting a nightingale.

One by one she lay there a long time, awaiting: a high branch of lilac was climbing the balcony (but) swaying there (rustling) interrupting: the Singeaut's dogs far away barking; and the mill throbbing so soft it might be thunder in Constantinople. She dimly (dreaming) while a corn-crake (digging in the field-perfume. Dimly) and:

Trains go thundering (under the white Seine cliffs yes?) distantly to Paris and the canalboats and (the Epte is it far away? (for example) that day when we all paddled down from Aveny?) and:

A cock's crowing throws a barbwire entanglement about the moon she thought (always at two o'clock) and the summer-blanketing air heaves in gauzy patters as (she and the pock-marked trees tossing restlessly) sleeplessly she thought:

This was where he walked. This was where he slept. This was where he drank calvados and played chess. This was where he made the bookshelves for me. This was where he (died?) From distant piers great ocean liners draw out; the bands all playing. And he has gone she thought:

Yet it is in the Seine at Paris nevertheless that all this lies mirrored: but (not for consolation) there is the low booming of the mill-wheel and people (playing an accordeon? . . . la valse brune. Les chevaliers de la lune. . . ?) going crinkling laughing homeward down past toward Monet's. He is in (New York?) she thought:

It is only sometimes these moods she remarked afterward but one second can split into millionths and at night (in the (dreaming) Giverny air) from her pillow the landscape tautens (rubberbandlike) to his feet wherever walking and she lay taut silent for a gesture cuts and (it snapping (one must accustom one's self?) recoiling) where she in this cupped town: and the night:

◆

But I above through the plaited roofs from the hillside I (my eyes like a diver's pointed hands) saw: .

My eyes saw:

Saw the white body:

The white body opening woundlike in the darkness:

The white body featherlike drifting:

The white body a compass needle swaying:

The white body a web across the couch:

The couch in the studio:

The studio where I had drunk calvados I had made book-shelves I had slept I had played chess:

I think dreams:

(One must accustom one's self?)

◆

There was a rush of air as she raised her head and her hair circling out across continents

◆

1. He walked into the room porcelain-green from yesterday's twilight and showing his badge the clerk with two eyes like coffee-spoons over a glassy counter—"Send this telegram to Police Headquarters, New York"

◆

2. Thomas K. Merkle and wife walking home on South Water Street Hungerford, N. J. from the Photoma Palace where they had seen 'Broken Bonds' starring Tom Mix and

Bessie Love a Paramount Feature were suddenly started in the quiet night by a loud roaring buzzing seeming to be approaching rapidly from out the sky directly overhead.

"My God!" cried Mr. Merkle with great presence of mind pulling his wife under a tree whence looking up they presently discerned the gleaming body structure of an enormous aeroplane dashing earthward out of the night at a terrific speed.

For a moment Terror tugged at his gullet. Then with a sigh of relief Mr. Merkle (the machine was at this time he afterward testified so close that the features of the aeronaut could be clearly observed peering from behind his wind screen) saw the awesome object zoom suddenly upward clearing by a hair's breadth (so it seemed) the machicolated cornice of the Hungerford Hardware Supply Company Building. It vanished, headed roughly E. S. E.

After a moment spent in regaining their shattered equilibrium as well as in readjusting their garments disarrayed in the first frenzied leap for safety the good couple proceeded directly homeward and to bed. Mrs. Merkle however (so great had been the shock of the nocturnal apparition) for some days after was subject to sudden fainting fits followed by chills in the extremities racking headaches retching and vomiting of so severe a character that at one time her life was considered seriously to be in danger.

◆

3. Charles Dograr doubled the corner of Park Avenue and Fifty-Third Street and glanced back hastily to see if he were being followed. There were only a few hours left now. Somehow. . . . something . . . it was as if things were closing in. His own footsteps seemed but the echo of another's passage.

Behind him, the street was vacant. But down Park Avenue, toward the Grand Central, a man in a dark suit made his solitary way. Charles Dograr studied that expressionless back like a dog sniffing a trail. Things were closing in. When the sun is setting, a man's shadow goes before him. Was he being paced—not tracked—by the detectives?

But it (this sense, this illusion (if you choose (and as he tried to persuade himself) to call it) that gripped him) was subtler far than that. Rather the variables in his soul's equation were x-ing out at last, and that constant factor which before he had never comprehended he—at the moment of grasping it—was perceiving to diffuse itself in the aura of another's personality; to dissolve itself in the flux of some unseen will stronger than his own as (some dream-personage unremembered. . . . ?) (throbbing black and white needle-like. . . ?)—if—(blue signs . . . ?) the energy of (blue waters. . . ?) another's purpose were infusing slowly, inexorably into his own.

Charles Dograr (again) thought it was God. (Again) he was wrong.

And now, doggedly, he sets his way in the footsteps of the man in the dark suit ahead.

There are only a few hours left now.

◆

4. A glare of dusted illumination, shuttling over a kaleido-scope of green and blue and yellow, spiraling round a spreading oval pearled with laughing faces and then sprayed waterspout-like up to the crossed tangle of cordage, the bellying convexities of the Big Tent. Thuds, cries, the taut march of a panther, a deep-throated growl followed by a spring as the Miraclomas, in the center ring, put the big cats through their act.

Mechanically, Adeline Laggick stepped aside in the run-way as the Eight Turners herded their twelve white horses out toward the wagons, even now preparing for departure. Their act was over. Hers was yet to come.

The streaking aerial silvered figures, the smell of sawdust calcium jungle-fur greasepaint manure sweaty clothes bran, the glazed hat of the ringmaster, applause, the gilded parade, the deep-set night pallor. . . .

She turned with meditative eyes to the face of Les' Din-kle, a clown, grinning cheerfully at her beneath the grotesque makeup.

"Are you married, Les'? Have you any children?" she asked impulsively, with the naïveté new to her.

The clown's face grew suddenly grave.

"Yes," he replied slowly, "I'm married, Ad'. Married to the gamest little woman this whole world holds. And kids. . . ? Say, I've got seven of 'em, countin' the twins, and take it from me, you can't beat 'em. Here, I'll show you a picture of the young-est. Always carry it with me.

But even as he fumbled in the voluminous folds of his costume, a bell clanged behind him. On the instant, with the instinct of an old 'Trooper,' he stiffened, forgetting all else.

"My 'turn,' Ad'," he exclaimed. "Show you another time." And he was off, tumbling and stumbling as, with sidesplitting mimicry, he played the part of a policeman in pursuit of an equally amusing burglar.

Adeline watched a moment. A telegram was thrust into her hands. Opening, she read: "Met me Erie Pa tonight twelve. Am on the trail. Cousin Herbert." She gasped.

The bell clanged. Her crimson cloak dropped from the lovely shoulders, revealing the tracery of gold and gauze that adorned but not concealed her quivering figure. Sidling sidewise, hips swaying, she advanced under the hot glare of a hundred incandescents to do her last 'turn.'

But even as the flageolet and tambourine throbbed in a desert love song—even as the bangles clashed and shivered, shimmering in the rotating movement of her high-swinging breasts—even as the dance grew wilder and the strings of imitation pearls about her hips swished and clattered at the retching looping of her toggling loins and the rosette of pink ribbon sewn just below the small of her back flapped and quivered with the rhythmic revolving of her behind and her whole body was rippling and trembling, the very incarnation of unlicensed desire—even then and through it all, till she stood, spent and panting, listening to the roar of applause at the impassioned finale—the words of that telegram, borrowing the cadence of the dance, were repeating themselves in her mind: "Meet me Erie Meet me Erie Meet me Pa. tonight. Meet me twelve tonight Meet Me."

Once, the tones of the clown, too, came to her as with unstudied insincerity he had told her of his wife and kiddies. But she had put that aside. Hardly waiting for an encore, she skipped, all flushed and beautiful, to the exit.

Then a glance at her watch. Ten-forty-five. She could just make it.

◆

5. Two men in the turmoil of the noon crowds at Grand Central converging. They brush shoulders. A quick handclasp; unnoticed a scrawled slip of paper is thrust into waiting fingers. Unnoticed? Charles Dograr had been right behind. Without a moment's delay, he followed the larger of the two, a tall heavy-set blonde man wearing a derby hat. Outside, the man leaped into a waiting motor car. Charles stayed long enough to notice that the license plate bore the insignia of the New York Police Department. Then, giving the driver orders to "follow the car ahead" he leaped into a waiting taxicab. Both were swallowed up in the traffic of Forty-Second Street.

◆

6. The ticket-seller in the railway station of a small country town looked out through his grating at the flushed, thickly painted feminine face that moved into line with his, then down

at the ten-dollar bill an exquisitely manicured hand had shoved across the counter.

"Yeou be one o' them there circus peepul, ain't ye, Miss?" he queries with half a leer.

"None of your god damned business!" replied the girl. "Give me a ticket to Erie, Pennsylvania."

◆

7. A chance phrase often reveals, in an unguarded moment, more a man's character than could hours of conscious analysis. The old gentleman known now to us as Picrolas once remarked: "A rose is loveliest in the parabolic moment when, decapitated by your walking stick, it sails for a yard or two through the sunlight and then falls, ruined, in the dust."

This idea, at once so beautiful and so repellent, withal so insouciant, illustrates more than any comment the forces at work in the old gentleman's mind at the moment:

He is seated at his desk (or table) in the window of his room at the lodging house on West Twenty-Third Street. He looks out on the street as if he heard (as indeed he does) some young men practicing the ukelele on the porch below.

Pen and paper lie before him. He is writing a poem, or a letter to Charles Dograr, or an apologia for his career (the facts were never clearly known). Suddenly he bursts into tears. His head falls forward on the desk. Heavy sobs rack his body.

Now his head rises from the couch of his crossed arms. His eye falls on the x-ray machine. A bitter sneer twists his lips, which form the words: "What—has—this—profited—me?"

He rises. He seizes a hammer. With a quick movement he swings it above his head; is about to bring it down on the delicate mechanism. A fit of coughing shakes him. He leans against the table for support till the spasm shall pass.

("Why? . . . Why? . . ." he gasped, like a [sic] infant wonderingly. A cold tentacle of phlegm lapped against his palate and a retching convulsion squirmed into his throat. For a moment he struggled literally for breath. "If–I can—last—long enough. Only a—few hours–more!")

Again the weight of hatred tautens his courage. He flings the hammer to a far corner of the room. He strides to the desk; tears up the paper on which he had been writing. For a moment he stares down into the street below. His back is turned to the camera, but his hands are seen to clench with rage. He turns, raises his fist above his head. His lips form the words: "Curse— Charles—Dograr! He—has—spurned–me!"

With extreme care, he begins polishing the glittering accoutrements of the machine.

(Iris out on the machine)

◆

8. A telephone girl at the switchboard. A light flashes. She plugs in.—"Long distance from Erie? Aw ri'. . . . Yeah, this Plice Headquarters. Whosi' for? . . . Huh? . . . the Chief? . . . Aw r' . . . Waitaminit. You'll get yeh connection." She plugs in the wire for the Chief's Office, twitches the call-bell lever.

13—LE KERMÈS DE L'YEUSE

In the studio they were all drinking but (as she stepped like falling out) on the balcony (behind her the treacherously lighted room a bomb in the night and) clutching the chill iron railing she:

(Inside weaving back and forth they laughing they were all dancing and singing Teddy Pierre Jim Lily they were all drunk) the stars like shark's teeth smiled at her. It is cool she felt and (patting down her breasts her breathing sides to the trickling flanks) the whiskbroom breeze as (inextricably intermingled with trees they were all drunk) tumbling (the light striped with laughter spread fanlike) they:

La viande qui   *here*   well
    put on that   here   *that's*   I like
c'est   BlueBlowers record   *my*   who's got
   pas   dance?   *'sais pas*   more punch?   *glass!*
rigolo   open that other   *bonnes d'enfant*
   maybe   baby   calvados
    baby maybe   don't mean   baby
       maybe

she here (if for a while no) no I am not (no one) not drunk but: her throat fluffed rigidly against that last glass of (sweetish: and her mind softening like a tremulously uprearing cone gelatinous) slightly painful but: it must be balanced:

(I shall not be drunk she thought: Where was he?) she thought:

(As with (almost) tears) here he died (as she remembering: Ah! It had been wonderful in the old days!) remembering: the arm behind her back his legs (hooked) into hers while (the night like a shawl about her shoulders and) the writhing filmy night. I said yes. I always (and) looking down:

It fell to earth and bred millions of little white moths about her eyes (I am not (crying I am not) drunk. He has gone) but:

It became four stories and kneading (the balcony becoming a window) into a tall brownstone old house: it would be a bedroom: it would be pinkshaded: the girl wears blue: and (carefully) adjusting (her head like the kermés de l'yeuse hardening) and her arms against the cold granite windowsill. She looks down as that other shall do four stories into (where was he? West Twenty-Third Street?) and:

It is West Twenty-Third Street so for a few minutes she offers up hours and hours of watching (before the next dance) a vicarious sacrifice to Love. She produced:

1. Late into the night, Hélène Montmorency remained at her window, staring across the light-lichened expanse of Twenty-Third Street at the House of Mystery opposite.

Sometimes the ripe red lips parted in a sigh. Sometimes a whisper, scarce louder than a sigh, issued from that perfect throat—"He will come soon now"—and, faintlier-flying than her swarming hopes, lost itself on the nigrescent air as she settled again (unconscious of that other who with deft fingers the creamy shoulder modeling, shaping the soft voluted throat across miles and her head dreaming) to the lonely vigil. And still the grim house across the way concealed its secret.

That there was danger she knew. So much she had read in the curl of Fred's predatory lips, in the exultation of his glance as, with scarce a word to her, he had dashed into the room, seized his pistol and hurried out to the street again.

There, from her window she had seen him—strangest sight of all on that strange night!— cross the street and disappear behind the heavy portal of the House of Mystery. And when, at last, he had reappeared, it had been arm in arm with that one–Charles Dograr as we know, his name to her unknown— to whom one night she had thrown sweet kisses and, breathless with passion, had seen him fling the honeyed swarm back from his lips to hers again!

Fred—with the man she loved! A thousand surmises sued her reason for a tardy credence. The man she loved, and the man who loved her, walking arm in arm together! Had Fred forsworn his duty? Had he been won over by bribes—by the cunning persuasion of that old gentleman whom she saw, from time to time behind his window, spiderlike at work among the webbed mechanism of his strange machine? Had he—but no! With all his faults, Fred Coolan prized above aught else the Honor of the Force. And besides, that Captaincy of Detectives—his dream for many years—he had said would be the guerdon of a successful capture. And that he suspected these two across the way of responsibility for the Electric Murders that had terrorized the city, there was no doubt.

Had he trapped them, then? Had he wormed his way cunningly into their confidence, that he might learn their plans and then betray them? If so, only a miracle at this late hour could save the youth she loved from destruction—or worse.

But rather, had they, by superior cunning, misled the detective and tangled his feet in the net of their persuasion? She watched and wondered, waited and watched. Three o'clock boomed from the Metropolitan Tower (or the mill, is it the Epte? pulsing across the fringing perfumed fields? she weaving?) waiting:

"He won't be long . . . now. . . ."

Love, of all the passions flesh is heir to—Love alone could furnish a flame so intense at once and so enduring, to keep those long hours warm with hope, alight with expectancy.

Hélène Montmorency, her body, soiled by contact with a world that is hard and dreary enough for the most fortunate of us, but to none harder, to none drearier than to an orphan foundling cast forth at an early age from the doors of a heartless institution instead of a mother's fond love, penniless, into a brutal world, had grown callous under Life's buffetings.

But deep in the inner core of her weary heart one shrine she had kept pure. And here now, as before an altar, she burned before his image the incense of her adoration.

"Soon . . . now." And shifting slightly in her cramped position as (carefully unfolding the satin fold of her kimono slipping revealing the snow-white softness of that matchless shoulder, the incipient curve of the lifting breasts and like moons in syzygy the crescent curves of thigh and abdomen where scented like pineapple, downy-fragrant like fields cupped beneath the strobile night and with soft weaving fingers modeling as (there are people crinkling laughing on the road "I shall look like a storm here staring white" and still down) waiting:

Sense ye not, Hélène Montmorency, that silent watching figure—miles, miles away, 'tis true, in flesh, but near, so near, in dream and thought? Feel ye not, Hélène Montmorency, those weaving fingers, softly threading thy marble-veined limbs with life, cushioning thy proud, ripe breasts within the silken shift and offering all, in the amorous Night, to the distant lover?

And you, Charles Dograr, danger forgotten, the chase forsaken, the lust of gold, the heat of passion stilled at last—what hidden Will now leads you back down the silent street and makes you pause a moment, unnoticing, beneath a certain window ere you cross and enter, to join the erst loved, now hated, companion of your many crimes?

◆

2. He stands a moment in the silent street. A bit of paper flutters down before him. Opening, reading: "*Beware of the blonde man!*" His features express surprise. He looks up. All the windows of the house are dark, tenantless. Shaking his head, as one confronted by an insoluble riddle, he crosses the street. Lets himself into Mystery House with latchkey.

◆

3. Within an upper chamber of the House Across The Way, a girl in a blue silk chemise kneels by her bedside. The room is dark. Only a single moonray, stealing through the open window, illuminates the sobbing shoulders, gilds like an aureole the straying, silken hair.

She is praying and, as she prays, scalding tears flow streaming down the shell-pink cheeks. She raises her eyes, her clasped hands to Heaven. Her face, torn by emotion, moves convulsively. Her lips form the words: "Save—him—from—danger."

Fade-out

◆

4. Press-room of metropolitan paper. Men hurrying to and fro with spiked sheets, rolling hogsheads of ink back and forth, etc. Foreman of press-room stands beside stopped presses, with order for make-up in his hand. Gesticulates angrily, looking at watch. Assistants surround him, deprecatory.

Caption:

"Half an Hour Past Deadline Now.
First Time The Paper's Been Held
Up In Years."

◆

5. City-room of paper. Rows of reporters at typewriters; eye shades; throw sheets of paper hastily into copy baskets.

Desk (R.U.E.) City Editor, shirt sleeves, smoking cigar, reading galleys. Looks at watch. Calls star reporter to his side.

Caption:
> *"How About That City Mercantile*
> *Bank Story? If We Hold The Presses*
> *Till Midnight And They Don't*
> *Make The Arrest. . . ."*

6. Reporter smiles. Hands sheet of typed paper to Editor.

Caption:
> *"Here's The Lead For The Story.*
> *The Chief Of Police Told Me They*
> *Have The Gang Under Their Thumb*
> *And They'll Pinch Them All When*
> *They Try to Rob The Bank. It's*
> *A Sure Thing."*

7. Editor looks doubtful. Shakes Head. Takes sheets from reporter; scans them; begins to smile approvingly.

8. *Close-up flash of story;*
> X-RAY MURDERER CAUGHT AT LAST
> Scientific Criminal and Accomplice
> Arrested on Threshold
> of Big Hold-Up

*One Hundred Shots Fired On Crowded
Thoroughfare. Police Make
Long-Awaited Arrest As
Thousands Stare.*

At an hour a little past midnight, as he stood surrounded by eighteen victims on the threshold of his greatest *coup*, René Fonstant, alias Benjamin Constantin, Thorndyke Smithers, Edouard Percy, James Butler, Arthur Moss, etc., etc., met justice at last.

Two police cars swung around a corner loaded with policemen, as he was transferring nineteen millions in specie from a looted armored car into a waiting motor car before the City Mercantile Bank, and after a furious pistol battle in which nine policemen and two bystanders were wounded, succeeded in putting under arrest the most dangerous and brutal murderer in the history of crime.

With him was his young accomplice, alias Charles Dograr. Both stand charged with the astounding total of sixty-seven murders, all committed—by means of some as yet unknown mechanism permitting electrocution by radio—within the short space of two months. They pleaded 'Not Guilty,' and it is said that eminent legal aid will be called in to their assistance in what promises to be one of the most sensational trials of the century. Fonstant himself, as he was. . . .

◆

9. Editor looks up from copy, smiling.

Caption:
> *"It's A Good Story. We'll Wait For It.*
> *Better Run Down To The Bank And Be On*
> *The Spot When They Pull It Off."*

◆

10. Steps of rooming house on West Twenty-Third Street. A fuzzy little man ascends to door, rings bell. Landlady opens. They talk.

Caption:
> *"Can I Get A Room Here, Ma'am?"*

Landlady opens door wider. He goes in, after hasty glance, as if one hunted, around and up and down street. It is Rupert Pragman.

◆

11. Solemnly (circling the hills and bluegray fields behind) Binghampton; Utica; Syracuse; Troy a man ploughing and (cleaving (a white road where the red and green buckboard spick-and-span is pawing) the horizon) and: *click-toc-toc-click-toc-toc-click-toc-toc-click*
From here and there scattering the lights went on: with

a shattering roar of wheels couplers grinding whirling axles following: between the dead blank walls of a factory Eastman's Soap. It was Amsterdam and on:

"When do we reach New York?"

"Well, boss, we was thutty minutes late outa Erie but we made up fifteen minutes already. Ah raickon we'll pull in awn time at tenfawty. Yessuh."

Herbert Trask, seated in the railway carriage, glances impatiently at his watch. Half past nine.

◆

12. Office of Chief of Police. Large, handsome man with irongray mustache. In uniform, seated at mahogany desk. Picks up telephone and twiddles hook. Then talks into receiver.

◆

13. Precinct police station. Police lieutenant at desk, writing in blotter. Several policemen tunics unbuttoned lounge in chairs. (It is a heavy-angled room as if it suspended tons of masonry and in an egg-yellow illumination; policemen always look as if they had just finished stew and dumplings for dinner and these in the scene their faces belch at the vacant walls) Lieutenant answers phone. Speaks, nodding deferentially —Yes, yes, yes. Snaps receiver back on hook, summons policeman.

Caption:
> *"Stand By For A Riot Call. Chief Says*
> *They're Going to Pinch Them Radio*
> *Murderers Tonight!"*

◆

14. There was a knock on the door. Hastily concealing his test-tubes in a drawer and (throwing a cloth shrouding the outlines of the x-ray machine—"Come in," the old gentleman called and) the door opening.

A smallish man his face emerging from a light fuzzy gray suit like a moth from its cocoon was standing there. He was casting quick furtive glances at the apparatus of the room.

"Well?" and a suspicion Worcestershire-sauce-like the old gentleman at his heart as—"Is. . . . is this the . . . ah . . . Seaside Employment . . . Agency?" The man's voice ran down the words like a timorous spider down its thread.

"No!" barked the old gentleman. "I'm busy."

The little man hesitated.

"I'm busy. Get out!"

But for a long time afterward. . . .

◆

15. "This is the last time," he had said. He had gone away and left her. Running with brilliant rapidity through her mind in the short space between the Manager's Office and her

dressing room, Adeline Laggick had lived over again the events of that afternoon on the Palisades, spent in the arms of the man she now knew to be her uncle's murderer.

Her flesh crawled as she thought of it . . . his kisses . . . faugh! (She wipes her lips at the remembrances, expressing disgust) . . . the nestling tug of his hip into hers . . . this man, this Dograr, as Herbert had said he called himself—was a coward, a cur, and yet . . . was it true, what the doctor had said—that she would bear a child to this monster? . . . Would she pay the price of the shameful thing she had done on that moon-darkened evening? . . . Oh! . . . And children. . . . Les' Dinkle . . . What was it he had said? . . .

So, her face gray and weary beneath the greasepaint . . . and here Dinkle himself, waiting sheepishly before the door of her dressing-room. . . . Good old Les' . . . Her heart warmed at his honest eyes. . .

"I was waitin' to show you that snap o' my youngest kid, Ad," he brought out awkwardly. And added, still more sheepishly. "Say, Ad! I was figurin' out a darn' good number you an' me could do together—supposin' . . ." he hesitated painfully. . . . "Supposing you an' me was to . . . you know . . . get married an . . . go into vaudeville together. . . ." He looked beseechingly up at her.

"But you're already married aren't you, Les'?" she queried, wondering.

"Aw, sure . . . but my wife's a Mormon. We was married out in Salt Lake."

A sudden revulsion seized her. Men were all alike. And this

Dograr. . . . Once she had thought. . . . But she could not bring herself to hurt this honest heart.

"We could try it out here . . . you know . . . work it up with the circus before we jumped."

"It's too late for that, Les'," she answered sadly. He stared in amazement. "I got the can five minutes ago."

"You! Fired! Why, but listen. . . ." he was stuttering, sobbing, in his mingled wrath and amazement. "Listen, Ad', you got your contrac'."

"Evans says it's cancelled. You see, I jumped the show last night, to—to meet my cousin in Erie, Pa."

"Aw, but say, Ad'. . . ."

It wrenched her heart. But the mission now before her . . . she must purge herself of all the softer passions . . . she must forge her mind, her body to the instrument of Hate. For a moment sorrow blinded her eyes and she stared with infinite compassion at the honest face before her. Then—

"It's too late, Les'. I'll remember you. Good-by. Good-by!" A wrenching handclasp, tearing her soul—and his. She was gone!

14—MIDNIGHT

The City Mercantile Bank on Warren Street is one whose name figures small indeed in the financial activities of a city whose bank clearances often exceed a billion dollars daily.

Founded in 1802, it still remains in the modest, though solidly-constructed building of brick and brown-stone, while its more prosperous brothers rear skyscraper temples and scatter branch agencies, glittering with brass and glass, throughout the city.

In the City Mercantile the accretion of 127 years has produced only a slightlier musty tang in the unhurried atmosphere, a deeper polish on the worn and furrowed mahogany of the counter fittings and (seemingly) a more rheumatic curve in the bent backs of the tellers at their windows and of the clerks in the counting room. Everyone seems old there.

But though its whole equipment be fifty years out of date; though its personnel abound in quinqua- (even septua-) genarians; though it make no attractive offers to gain new depositors, yet there still flows a goodly volume of money through the worn gratings of its teller's windows.

For, at its founding, James R. Stacker, its first president, was a power in the then financial world of New York. Came readily to him as clients the then most influential business houses of the day. And though many of these have fallen in the rising tide of competition, there are many as well who have thrived and prospered in the century's passage.

And of these, all—through regard for the unflinching honesty of an unbroken line of Stackers at its head; through perhaps a touch of sentiment at the thought of the old bank's history—have continued as clients of the City Mercantile.

It will be seen, then, that the City Mercantile Bank occupies a position unique in the financial world. Its list of clients is small, but immensely wealth. Its transactions, though infrequent, are always for immense sums. Its vaults, though pitifully antiquated, are alternatively empty, or bursting with huge gold deposits.

Couple this with an ingrained obstinacy among its personnel, from President Stacker down to the aged doorman, against new methods—credit them with an utterly unjustified conviction that the crime problem of the modern city is as simple as it was in the year 1805, and it will readily be understood that the 'cannon' (vice: 'stick-up man'—'highwayman') spoke truth when he said "I could take a brass band along and lift the works!"

◆

1. "I don't see why they don't come along and get this over with. All these guns and battleship armor-plate! Newfangled notions! Why, in my day. . . ." The hour was eleven-thirty. The speaker was James Miller, for forty-two years chief teller of the bank.

"Now, Mr. Miller," Henry Gray, the night watchman

interrupts. Old in the service as the other, he permits himself many minor liberties. "Don't you go and get yourself all het up about it. You know they ain't due here 'till twelve, an' it's only ha'past eleven now. And listen here," he added as an afterthought, "You jus' go inside an' set down where it's warm 'f you don't want to get your rheumatiz' back again! Standin' outside in this night air!"

"You shut up, Henry Gray! I'm not worrying about my rheumatism when I got nineteen millions in gold pieces to get off my hands." Nevertheless he turns back to the interior where a portable oil stove has been lighted in the lobby of the bank, to warm the watchers. Around its cheery glow five men are grouped—four special policemen and Mr. Blodgett, the assistant teller. The youngest of the group, he is 47 years old, has served in the World War and has been twice decorated for bravery under fire. We shall hear more of him later. The others, stretching their gnarled old hands out to the flames, the old jaws working rhythmically over the individual 'chaw' of tobacco, look more like a chatty group of codgers gathered beside some country stove, than the guardians of a treasure surpassing the wildest dreams of avarice.

Only the rifles, stacked in the corner against the counter, and the cavernous, shadowy interior lend a sinister touch to the scene.

"What time is it, Blodgett?" asks Miller. "I swan, boys, I feel oneasy [sic] tonight, I do. Like as if something untoward was about to happen."

◆

2. Charles Dograr rises from the chair-arm lunch and fending aside the reverberating brilliance of the indigestible tile walls he makes his way to the (it is cool dark on the slippery pavement and) the long loop of Lexington Avenue. A motor car has drawn to the curb. He steps on the running board, climbs in as with gathering speed it turns down Twenty-Second Street:

◆

3. An instant of blackness. The side curtains are down. The glow of a cigarette against a blued jaw:

Caption:
> *"Where Is The Blonde Man?"*

Nobody seems to answer and the man negligently puffing a lungful of smoke and there is a kind of murderous waiting amusement in his attitude.

Caption:
> *"Aw, He Said He'd Meet Us Downtown."*

◆

4. But one would swear the air is shaking are they laughing?

The traffic lights on the Avenue switch to red. Smoothly the car swerves into a side street. "What time is it?"—"Twenty minutes to."

5. With a sweep and a (sidewise) bumping. To the eye of its bluecoated occupant the wings strumming steady and: the world oscillates and especially (the Times Square Building like a top-heavy pendulum swinging between black roofs) the electric signs: the Y of rushing streetway. Swiftly the airplane rises: circles: speeds south.

◆

6. A flash to the old gentleman in the still room: the light like butter smeared across the angled jaw. All passion chills against the eyes (like icicles) etching the machine against the yellow walls. His hands softly moving adjusting. Slowly the swiveled barrel swings. It hums. The ray moves out.

He smiles (but his smile shattered by a cough and) a bitter horror. His gaze steadies triumphant. Again to the oculascope.

Caption:
> *With Infinite Care He Centers The*
> *Mechanism On His Intended Victims.*

7. A shuttling sweep of windows blinking as (the spurt of people hurrying (among them Herbert and Adeline) and) EXPRESS SOUTH FERRY. They are jammed aboard and (gleaming down the black nozzle (shimmering with darkness)

of the tunnel) where the red lights disappearing.

"Are we in time?" she had cried. For a moment his strong arm had held her; his eye gazed into hers. "Oh! Herbert! Avenge me! His death alone can purge my body of its shame! Avenge me, and I am yours—all yours!" And leaping together.

◆

8. Fred rushes in on Hélène. She, watching, has only time to hear his half-uttered cry of exultation before: his feet tumbling downstairs in the quiet. One glance to the street. She leaps to her feet.

Caption:

"I Must Save Him!"

And hastily fastening a dress about her chilled form, a hat pushed over her tousled silky hair. She follows. Whither?

◆

9. "Here comes the armored car, Mr. Miller!" "Wha-what? Where?" He had been dozing. "Right outside now. They're unloading."

◆

10. The man in the airplane saw it all. Revolving slowly and the street like a magnetic needle pointing to an inconstant north

as it swung, he saw far down (and the buildings like inverted cones mutually intersecting) at:

The shiny-hard beetle-backed armor of the truck at the curb. It was exactly midnight. He saw the guards step out of the slotted doors. They spaced the vacant sidewalk. From the bank (seen above, circling) the bustling little figures with peeping feet and floating shoulders. Four special policemen a man in a gray uniform a man in a brown a man in black in diminutive eddies around where:

A door has swung open. The sacks are dumping out. The man in the airplane sees it all and hastily dot-dot-dashing the news to Headquarters where a man with an irongray mustache:

◆

11. Hélène slipping from doorway to doorway follows Fred down the street. He pauses at the corner. She, shrinking into a store entrance sees a gray car swoop to the curb. A moment's colloquy. Fred leaps in. Hastily she leaps into a waiting taxi. "Follow the car ahead!"

◆

12. And now in his cupola of silence the old gentleman he makes the last adjustment and chuckling:

Caption:
    "Charles Shall Die—Last Of All!"

His treacherous mirth. His eye settles to the oculascope. Like a snake to strike the whole coiled mechanism. His hand closes on the insulated lever. Down!

Caption:

"One!"

And (but before he again) he moves a switch and the Dead Plane cupping dimming over his (one sees moving spidery within the Plane) his face white opaque as:

◆

13. No one had seen that the driver of the armored truck but: and his hands as if taking away. A kind of liquid blueness his face. Unobserved, a powerful motor car quietly stealing had crept abreast the truck on the opposite side of the street. Charles Dograr leans out. Across the way and a guard whirling; his hand drops to the holster but: like a kick in the forehead and: as if a box of matches igniting all at once his face. Charles laughed aloud. All turned.

◆

14. To explain why, at this particular moment, Mr. Thomas K. Merkle should have decided to walk down Warren Street we must recall to the reader's mind the fainting, choking, vomiting fits to which his wife had been subject, and which had been

induced, in all probability, by the strange airplane which had swooped down over them the previous night in Hungerford, N.J., and vanished. In further justification of what may seem at first an unpermissible [sic] coincidence, we may state that inventory-taking at the plumbers'-fittings store in which Mr. Merkle worked had necessitated late hours among its clerks— and that Mr. Merkle had promised, on returning homeward, to stop at an all-night drugstore on Warren Street to get a prescription filled, before taking the ferry.

He saw ahead of him, fulcruming the tilted, deserted street, the blue-painted racer, the big black truck standing side by side. He noticed, wondering, the moving group of figures, the opened bank doors. And, darting with a spurt of terror through his bewilderment, with a glance overhead he made out the dim-shining wing-structure, heard the muffled roar of the airplane circling overhead.

"What's up, I wonder?" Mr. Merkle asked himself. The question was never answered. As he advanced, he saw a man fall; sprawl grotesquely on the sidewalk. It was a man in a black suit. Another reached; leaned; crumpled. A man with a brown belt over a blue uniform skipped toward the shelter of the truck, tugging at his belt; then as if he had suddenly gone lame and pitched into the gutter. There was also a man in gray lying on the bank steps. Another. Another.

Dimly, Merkle realized that he was present at a holocaust. But he saw no firing, heard no shots. Across the street, leaning out of the racing car, a young man was watching, smiling.

Merkle suddenly wanted to run, to shout, to hide, to hit the young man's smiling lips. At the same moment, paralyzing all motion except his slow onward stepping came the flash: "It's the Electric Murderers!" and "Mary's tonic! I must get out of this!"

A man came out of the bank door as if he had been thrown out; his body slammed down in an ungainly heap at the foot of the steps. Two young men had climbed out of the racing car, were leisurely loading heavily-padlocked sacks from the truck into the tonneau of their car. The smiling young man was lighting a cigarette.

Merkle realized he had not yet been noticed. A frenzy of fury began to mount in his heart. Like a man pointing a gun, deliberately, he aimed his wrath at the young man. The airplane's roar overhead was diminishing. No one was in sight. Midway of the street the two gunmen and the sack they were carrying dropped lumping together.

At this, the young man standing still, now alone, beside his car, became oddly audible. Merkle comprehended that it was laughter. His rage soared to his arms like wings. From behind the armored car he plunged full on the defenceless Charles Dograr.

Charles had not even time to raise his arms. He saw the contorted face, the flailing arms flung suddenly at him out of blackness—saw the apparition sweep at him, full of vengeful life—saw the head jam sidewise in mid-career—and was nearly overturned as the lifeless body slumped heavily against him, tottered, and fell slowly at his feet. There was a blue mark on the forehead!

For a moment, Charles was too confused to reason. "Eighteen! Eighteen!" he murmured slowly. "But then this man. . . . Why is the old gentleman aiming this way? . . . If this guy hadn't come in between . . . pushed me back. . . . Why, he's already got his. . . . Why . . . why . . . the old murderer must–have—been–aiming–at—me!" The conclusion was obvious.

"*At me!*"

And then, as with the snap of a switch, he was galvanized into sudden furious energy. If the old gentleman was (as indeed he had been) aiming the x-ray gun at Charles, there was no time to be lost. He leaped to the driver's seat, threw in the gear. The car swung grinding round the corner and away.

A moment later, the gray police car hurled into the deserted street.

Fred, standing braced against the windshield gave a hasty glance around; cursed.

"They got away!" he cried. The car swooped to the corner. Far, far up Broadway, he saw the speeding fugitive. "There he goes! Give her the gas, Jim!"

◆

15. "Nineteen!" With a horrible chuckle, the old gentleman leans back from the mechanism as: and with like thunder cries: as—the door hammering. He reaches for the Dead Plane lever. There is not time! A tall stranger a painted flashing girl through the split panels. An X of tugging hands over the lever. Slowly, the old gentleman's feebler fingers give way.

"Where has he gone?

"Who?"

The girl sweeps between, her face afire with hate. "You know who! Dograr! Your pal!"

The man draws her away. "Wait, Adeline. He'll tell." His eye grows menacing. "He'll tell, or. . . ."

The old gentleman laughed. "Tell?" he cackled. "Why shouldn't I tell?" For a moment his old voice broke, sobbed. "Dograr—is—dead!"

Adeline burst into a wild laugh. "I wish I thought so!" she cried, and to the tall man: "Come on, Herbert, don't let him get away with that."

But Herbert had been watching intently. "I think he believes it, Ad," he said. "I think he thinks he killed him. . . ."

The old man's voice cut in, rising to a thin shriek. "Never mind who killed him. He's dead. . . ."

Herbert's fist came down. "Listen, old man. Charles Dograr is driving like mad up Avenue B at this present moment. I know what happened. You aimed your infernal machine to blast the brain of your partner, but at the instant you closed the switch, a man stepped between. You killed Thomas K. Merkle, of Hungerford, N. J.! Charles Dograr is alive!"

"Charles Dograr is alive!"

"Charles Dograr is alive!"

Again the girl, a fury of revenge. "And we want to know where he's gone to. We want to know! You'll tell us, by God! or . . . or. . . ."

The old gentleman had been regarding her half-smiling.

"Why," he asked, "why do you want to know where he is?"

Perhaps she sensed the common feeling between them. Abruptly, she ceased her threats.

"Because I hate him," she replied. "He was a beast—yes! worse than a beast to me! I have sworn to kill him!"

"I hate him too," replied the old gentleman simply, wearily. "You will find him at my country house—Greenwood Manor, Bayslip Road, Long Island."

"Straight?"

"I swear—it!" A slight cough had shaken the feeble voice.

"Come on Herbert!" She turned with a whirl of draperies toward the door.

"Wait!" They paused. The old man, his face clenched over his agony, seemed to speak. A fit of coughing plugged his throat a moment. Then—

"Go by—the Queens—Bridge. Take–the—Flushing cut-off. You'll catch–him. Kill. . . ."

He waved a hand wearily at them. They were gone, like prestidigitation. He turned, half falling, slumped over the light-box of the machine. Here it was as if his arms and hands exploded. A hammer, the uprooted switch, and his nails clawing at the wires of the antennæ. He struck; pounded, hammered; here, there; brandishing.

(The machine lies in ruins. The old gentleman, pale, staggers; flops inert across the shattered mechanism. A trickle of red flows wormlike from a corner of his mouth, drips silently on the x-ray barrel. Stillness).

◆

16. The man in the airplane saw it all—saw the two cars speeding up the broad reaches of Avenue B, the gray car now gaining, now falling slowly back again as the man crouched low at the wheel of the leading car, the wind like milk slashing past the windshield, he pulls open the throttle another notch. He saw the taxi, floundering in the wake of all, saw the girl (Hélène) leaning frantically from the door, crying: "Follow! Follow! Ten—twenty dollars if you follow them!"

They roar to the Bridge, sweeping up the broad approaches. He glides, circling over the high stone towers as they shuttle through the network of struts and girders and emerge roaring down toward Jackson Avenue and the straightaway out the Island. There, as on a map, they lie below him. He sees the spurt of flame as the man (Fred leaned out, braced against the windshield.—"I'll get the bastard!"—Aimed. Fired. Missed. The car sped on. Fred reloaded. "Step on it! Damn it! Step on it!")

And behind them both, the crawling taxi still hung on. He sees, too, looping swiftly across fields to the Flushing Cut-Off, the fourth car, a man at the wheel, a girl by his side—sees it leap across the chord of the arc the three other cars are following.

He sees the taxi stop, the girl climb out. ("Dis car won't go no foider, miss."—Frantic, she thrusts a roll of bills into the driver's hands. She takes to the fields, running madly blindly to her lover's aid. Rain is beginning to fall. In the darkness heavy like a weight on her shoulders, and she stumbles, falls, staggers to her feet again cut, bruised; she runs on. The wind whips her skirt against her legs; her jacket, her blouse sodden with rain clings chokingly about her. With frenzied haste "Will I be in time?"—She tears them from her, flings aside the trammeling garments. Clad only in her blue silk chemise, braving cold and sleet and darkness, sobbing panting crying, Hélène Montmorency races toward the man she loves!)

He sees the red car, slipping down the side roads converging, gaining now, and the gray car. Will the flying leader reach his goal in time?

◆

17. He lay where he had fallen. That yellow room the flat paneling of light dropping to the silent figure and his heart (or is it the tapping stick McDowell?) tap-tapping faintlier as: the old gentleman's eyes like glued paper curling open. In the doorway is that a human figure? Pragman turns his wiry nose about the doorjamb. He steals into the room. He prowls nervously to the old gentleman. ("Now this is a funny mess. What are these prongs for, I wonder? I always had a leaning for machinery. . . . And here's a little button, too. . . .")

He pressed the button. With a dull roar the building swaying, swept up in a praying fan of light and Pragman: the old gentleman and: as the explosion shattered: McDowell tap-tapping smiling and: it settled in a crumpled steaming dusty pile of rock and masonry.

◆

18. In a silent room at Headquarters. The Chief stops pacing a moment, pausing beside the desk of the radio operator, the instrument ticking.

"What's the latest, Ed?"

"Dograr making out for the center of the Island. Coolan gaining fast. A red car cutting in on Dograr. Toss-up whether Dograr or the red car gets in first."—A fresh outburst of ticking activity from the instrument.—"Here's news, Chief!" cries the operator excitedly. "The old guy on Twenty-Third Street just blew the house up! Total ruin!"

Expressionless, somber, the deep eyes of the Chief stare out toward where three fast cars are racing for the stakes of Life or Death!

15–BESIEGED!—DELIVERED!

He was running and before the (dim marble staircase like a dissected laugh) houndlike leaping the long corridor had faded into inkily black (and below knock-knock they are) hammering like the throbbing in his brain. His flash-light at last scalloping huge draping walls as doors as (and below if the door they are hammering if it holds firm?) pleating the beam of his light with shadow at last the stairs. The stairs to the tower.—"If I can reach the tower!"

Downstairs the heavy door with a crash of paneling. Like a cat his body crouching in the darkness his feet pivoted for flight he hears the searchers' voices.—"God! I near broke my get your guns ready boys went up this we got him close you look in that Harry no. Up this. Now!" And outside in the silence a sandpaper grate of gravel on the drive a skirl of brakes as wheels spin to a stop. More were arriving! Moments would swing the issue now!

Bolting the tower door and in the feathery darkness he felt stop by step mounting as his head through cobwebs. There was a stir of batwings in the deep-recessed walls. Something brushed heavily against his face. Behind below he heard their feet pounding as they searched the rooms. Nearer. His head came sharp against the flat wood. But he was beyond pain now. With a frenzied shove, the trap door swung upward and like a silver screen the sky. He was on the tower roof at last. And there:

Or (was it the breeze?) some dark woman distantly moving as her hair inwinding, her perfumed hair fine-netted enfolding and he:

Across continents some woman (the sky? or whose? those blue ingurgitating eyes?) voicelessly calling some woman beside blue waters undreamed-of melancholy-moving and or that low blue laugh the Seine?

As if the silver mail of her remembrance (the moonlight?) encrusting him. He felt the air warm like the pressure of her (he was asking?) breasts. Her breasts soft and warm and pointed and he felt (it was all about him) and as if (those enwinding hairs had they threaded deep in the veins of his body?) with a toss of her head he was swaying but across continents:

◆

The man in the airplane (his hand gripping hard on the lever that would release the bomb) he saw it all. He saw the tower top a gleaming disk a reflecting moon among the slope-shadowed angles of the gables. He saw (a dark effigy on the silent tower) the waiting figure of the man they hunted. As he circled and rose again, he saw the dozens of patrolling men, their figures black against the moondusted lawn, saw occasionally the light flash along the barrels of the guns they carried.

To the rear of the house, the red car had nosed deep in the tree-shadows. There a man and a woman, both with pistols ready, sat silent intense waiting their eyes fixed on the vacant windows of the building thenceforth to be known throughout the countryside as the "House of Dograr's Doom"!

He circled again, and Charles saw the wing surfaces gleam a moment, heeling into the turn, saw the machine drift downwind black like a bat against the moon, saw it swing round again heading stiffly up again to pass (and lower now) over his head.

Charles watching the thrumming monster, his throat choking. Then—a spit of flame from the hedgeshadow—a whipsnap crackle—the singing hiss of a bullet. It flattened against the wall below him. A woman's voice rose clear, exultant:

"Did I get him, Herbert? Did you see?"

A heavy bitterness swung like a pendulum in his stomach. He could not repress a cry:

"Adeline! Adeline!"

Another shot was the reply. And—"Stick your head up, you carrion! I'll give you Adeline!"

That voice . . . and she . . . he had thought.

Things accelerated. They were firing now on all sides. The air was full of bullets. His ear was vibrating with their hissing passage, the flack of impact. He could duck them, yes. But how duck that roaring approaching enemy from above, driving slowly back and forth in ever-tightening spirals overhead? How evade the bombs he knew it carried? And how elude (they were tearing the panels of the tower door below, he heard them hammering) those searchers in the house below, converging toward his hiding place?

Charles Dograr, even as he watched, knew there was no escape. He had but to wait . . . as bravely as he might . . . for annihilation. One thing the fighting Dograr blood assured him: he would never be taken alive!

"I shall die like a man!" he cried, with a clear eye for his Fate. "Say that I died game, boys!" he called down to the policemen massed below. A faint sound of cheering came up to him. But:

"You'll die like the dog you are!" he heard the voice of Adeline crying with vengeful hate. He saw her white hand raised, saw the pistol levelled.

"Shoot, girl!" he cried, stepping forward to the parapet. "Shoot! In the name of the child I gave you! My life for his!" And fearless, his hair atoss with the gentle breeze, his shirt thrown open across his breast he stood there, waiting, for the blow that would lay him low.

Even Adeline, heart-sore with hate as she was, must pause at sight of such magnificent courage as was his. And that moment cost her dear. Even as, at last, the gun in the girl's fair hand spat forth its leaden messenger of death, a crash, a rush of footsteps on the tower behind him made Charles Dograr turn. What new danger was this? Adeline's bullet, forgotten, sped harmlessly over his head. From the mouth of the tower stairway, all blue and pink and beautiful, burst sobbing panting in the open moonlight to fling herself wildly into his arms—Hélène Montmorency come to cover his lip's last life with kisses, to shield with the warmth of her fair body that of her lover— Hélène Montmorency beautiful and unashamed in the curving redundancy of her body's loveliness beneath the unconcealing silk chemise!

"Girl! girl!" (as he and with a voice like a phonograph but

yielding to those distant weaving fingers he)—"What madness brings you here?"

"Charles! My love! My life! My soul! I could not stay without you. If it be not fated that we live and love together, then grant me this, my last request, that we die—yes, die! here, together!"

She fainted. Still holding her throbbing form pressed close to his as he covered her lips with kisses and raising his eyes to Heaven and but:

(It was as if his eyes diamonds and from a thousand facets his vision gleaming on a world split in as many subtly-varying aspects; example: he perceived for the first time that of this touching scene of which he was the protagonist the background (viz., the ivy-mantled tower the stone-buttressed walls the hoary trees the lawn velvety to the tread) could be all dismantled at a moment's notice and as when (the showman politely bowing) the curtain rolling up on its mandrel disclosing the:)

And as even Fred too, then, the burly blonde man. His face black with passion. His eyes like coals with rage. He leaped heavily up the stairs and to and thrusting between them:

"You hound! I've caught you at last! Stand back, Hélène! It's he and I alone now! To the death!"

And but Charles with a vague deprecatory gesture (to be sure (he wonderingly) this girl in my arms now her half-opened lips the lidded eyes back-falling head the swaying back against my sustaining arm all firm, caressing to the touch and her hips (Again that sad gray woman beside blue waters phantom-moving he saw and the deepswimming eyes the weaving viviparous fingers) distant, unremembered he; yet yes! he almost saw her yes clear and threading this fair lovely figure sobbing against my breast as) with a brusk movement (it was as when a swimmer from deep water rising his head through the shell of dreaming darkness and his eyes glazed with light) for a moment bursting but:

The effect upon Charles was narcotic in the extreme. Or perhaps better than by the metaphor of the light-struck swimmer, we can describe his sensations in that curious moment by asking the reader if he (or she) have ever (seated through the indolent afternoon by some smooth-flowing river's side) seen suddenly a fish (fringe-jawed barbel, slim-backed trout—it matters not) leap from the current, arch gleaming, and disappear again? It was a spurt of foaming water—a silver twisting flash against the brush-covered bank—and, almost before the eye can have caught the picture, a plashing plunge—a thrust of the sturdy tail–and it has gone beyond pursuit, skimming the reedy river-bottom, and only the ripples repercussively lapping the bank beneath our feet remain to attest its passage.

Figure then, that the first is Charles as we the watchers; consider the arching moment through what to us was sunlight is, to him, blackness; remember that—as to us, plunging, the water which he starts—so to him the air we breathe, too long inhaled, spells suffocation and death; lastly, note that the spreading after-ripples which to us, rather than any actual vision of the leap, serve as basis by which we reconstruct in our mind's eye the finny apparition, remain to him only a swift-dimming, swift-narrowing cone of agitation, pointing deeper but fainter after him as he swims rapidly farther, deeper in (to the fish) the stream, or (to Charles Dograr) his dream.

But for Charles Dograr (as for the fish) that swerving flash through the uninhabitable land of remembrance had sufficed. Had sufficed to cool (as the fish its sides) his fevered imagining—had drained the heat of plot and counterplot from out his struggling soul. Though in the flashing moment he had been as one blinded by too much light, it had yet served to bring before him plain that Other Face—that gray, distant, dreaming woman. Like the lightning flash, its glare had been destructive, breaking the thread of her (to him unremembered) dream, freeing him forever from the almost corporeal imaginings that surrounded him and even as she (far-distant, dreaming) turned the last sheet and closed the book he was walking down Fifth Avenue, smoking a cigar.

END

EPILOGUE

And he. . . .
But and she:
Unaccountably, it was as she so often afterward used to tell, but then everything connected with the whole affair a conflict of unprobable [sic] impulses, she said: I only write adventure stories I don't want to live them, she said: give me the great open spaces of a Paris street, she said: let my eyes roam over the enormous vistas of the wallpaper in my room on the (and she always remembering: she walking the) rue Lacepède the rue (feeling smotheringly the smooth slipping of silk along the cool flesh of her thighs) Gracieuse the. . . .

It had been just a year. He was undoubtedly and yet he had said:

He had said. . . .

He had (Gentle Reader, we have seen her walking those old streets that fringe the Panthéon; we have seen her moody at the Seine-side, and sleepless in the Giverny air. Always her thoughts had been of him. And now) as:

(Yellowly the heat drip-drip-dripping from the funneling roofs) she held the sky over her head like an umbrella: he (had Oh! all that he) had said. But it had been just as she had supposed. New York too why hadn't she gone? But he had. . . .

It had been a year. She saw lait à volonté in a window and it closed her eyes with sudden tears: and down the rue du Puits-de-l'Ermite and turning. . . .

Glimpsingly she remembered she had (like the Kermés de l'Yeuse) imagined a granite windowsill on Twenty-Third: but had it had he: ah! were all men as. . . .

Sorrow corkscrewing she walking: she was remembering. . . .

◆

To the concierge with a fidgeting welcome:

"Bon jour Celestine."

"Bon jour Madame! And Madame returns so soon from the country?"

"Yes. I was bored." And, automatically: "No news, Celestine?"

And the other ducking in among the little room frying with sauté de veau she reappears with letters.

"Here are many letters for Madame."

She listlessly; but the other's barberish face beaming roguishly: "There is one letter from America. If it is from Monsieur Dograr?"

She could hardly contain herself. He had deserted her and: but he had said (a year) and hastily tearing open the envelop (all thought of concealing her perturbation thrown to the winds as the benevolent smiling the concierge) and all eyes as (ruffling to the signature):

"Yes! Yes! Celestine! It is from Monsieur Dograr after all!"

And then with trembling fingers the (maidenly) and she felt hot flushes mounting to her cheeks as (in his curious writing) here and there: ". . . have been thinking of . . . so much has . . . often wonder if after all I . . . curious sensation the other day. . . . I was walking . . . like a dream . . . overpowering. . . ."

And as the words ran together before the glad tears unnoticed streaming and the soft-hearted concierge. She found herself sobbing on the black alpaca shoulder.

"Oh! Celestine! Was ever happier woman than I? He–he–is coming back!"

Let us leave them thus.

1. The novel's playfully anarchic mood is established right at the start with the motto "Iunctis viribus molestum contempsimus," which was taken from Petronius Arbiter's satirical work *The Satyricon*. It can be translated as "joining forces we have despised that which is artificial, mannered, affected." Petronius's work was attractive to several artists of Coates's generation, among them F. Scott Fitzgerald, who proposed calling what became *The Great Gatsby* "Trimalchio in West Egg," or just "Trimalchio," after the ostentatious party-giver in Petronius's work, and T.S. Eliot, who also started *The Waste Land* with a quotation from *The Satyricon*. Whereas Eliot and Fitzgerald may have been stirred by the resemblance between the downfall of Roman civilization and the collapse of the modern Western world, Coates had little concern for the bankruptcy of old standards. On the contrary, the motto serves to underline the avant-gardist revolt against the labored, mannered, and artificial language of High Art.

2. The x-ray beam here actually embarks on a kind of surrealist performance; the reader joins the x-ray as it takes off on the kind of wandering spree that the surrealists engaged in as a way of seeing, in which erstwhile familiar objects assume new meaning and significance. Coates's comical use of random details in this list and elsewhere in the novel were clearly inspired by Dadaist and surrealist techniques.

The contemporary reader, meanwhile, will notice striking foreshadowings of postmodern novels like Thomas Pynchon's *The Crying of Lot 49* in that meaning is heavily suggested, clues are provided, but ultimately no answers or solutions are forthcoming.

Mathilde Roza is Associate Professor of American Literature and North American Studies at Radboud University Nijmegen, the Netherlands. She is the author of the critical biography *Following Strangers: The Life and Works of Robert M. Coates* (South Carolina University Press, 2011), which was based on extensive archival research. She has published on American modernism, *The New Yorker* magazine, and a variety of other topics.

The American novelist, short story writer and art critic Robert Myron Coates was born in New Haven in 1897. A graduate of Yale University, he traveled to Europe in the early 1920s and lived in Paris from 1921 to 1923. The great artistic turmoil that he witnessed there, from the activities of the Dada movement to Gertrude Stein's salon, inspired the young writer greatly, and left an indelible mark on his literary convictions. During his unusually varied career, he explored many different genres and styles of writing and produced three highly remarkable experimental novels, *The Eater of Darkness* (1926), *Yesterday's Burdens* (1933) and *The Bitter Season* (1946). He also wrote a historical novel, two crime novels, a book of memoirs, and two travel books about Italy. Simultaneously, Coates maintained a life-long career at *The New Yorker*, whose staff he joined in 1927. His starkly realistic and psychologically dark short stories of the 1930s and 1940s made a significant contribution to the magazine's developing stature as an organ for quality fiction. Also, from 1937 to 1967, Coates was *The New Yorker's* art critic and coined the term "abstract expressionism" in 1946. He was elected to the National Institute of Arts and Letters in 1958 and died in New York in 1973.

Group photo ca. 1900. The man in the first row is Coates's father. Robert Coates is to his left. The woman standing behind the young Coates is his mother. (Robert M. Coates papers, American Heritage Center, Laramie, WY)

Group photo ca. 1900. Coates holding the dog. (Robert M. Coates papers, American Heritage Center, Laramie, WY)

Robert Coates during his training for ROTC at Yale, 1917 [?]. (Robert M. Coates papers, American Heritage Center, Laramie, WY)

Group photo, members of Yale University Class of 1919. Coates the second from the right. (Robert M. Coates papers, American Heritage Center, Laramie, WY)

Group photo, 1920s, location unknown. Coates is second from the right. (Robert M. Coates papers, American Heritage Center, Laramie, WY)

Group photo, early 1930s, location unknown. Coates is second from the right. (Robert M. Coates papers, American Heritage Center, Laramie, WY)

Portrait of Robert Coates by Nina Hamnett, 1924

NOVELS AND BOOK-LENGTH WORKS

The Eater of Darkness. Paris: Contact Editions, 1926; New York: Macaulay, 1929.

The Outlaw Years: The History of the Land Pirates of the Natchez Trace. New York: Macaulay, 1930.

Yesterday's Burdens. New York: Macaulay, 1933.

All the Year Round: A Book of Stories. New York: Harcourt, Brace, 1943.

The Bitter Season. New York: Harcourt, Brace, 1946; London: Gollancz, 1949.

Wisteria Cottage. New York: Harcourt, Brace, 1948; London: Gollancz, 1949.

The Farther Shore. New York: Harcourt, Brace, 1955. Published as The Darkness of the Day. London: Gollancz, 1955.

The Hour After Westerly, and Other Stories. New York: Harcourt, Brace, 1957. Published as Accident at the Inn. London: Gollancz, 1957.

The View From Here. New York: Harcourt, Brace, 1960.

Beyond the Alps: A Summer in the Italian Hill Towns. New York: Sloane, 1961; London: Gollancz, 1962.

The Man Just Ahead of You. New York: Sloane, 1964; London: Gollancz, 1965.

South of Rome: A Spring and Summer in Southern Italy and Sicily. New York: Sloane, 1965.